WHISPERS

and
Other Strange Stories

Crina-Ludmila Cristea

Whispers and Other Strange Stories is an original work. No part of this book may be reproduced in any form or by any means, electronic or mechanical, without written permission from the author, except in the case of brief quotations embodied in critical articles and reviews. Reproducing and/or selling the material in this book without consent from the author is illegal and hurts the livelihood of both parties.

This is a work of fiction. All names, characters, places, and incidents are products of the author's imagination and any resemblance to actual people, places, or events is purely coincidental or fictionalized.

The author does not support nor encourage any sort of behavior or any acts that infringe on someone's well being, or that can be damaging to someone's body and mind.

This is a book for mature individuals only. Anyone who is easily scared, triggered, or offended, should think twice before reading because there are biting subjects explored within these stories and sometimes adult language is used to express certain ideas. Proceed with caution and expand your imagination.

First edition published independently in 2019.

Cover art by Vanessa Tavares aka Psyca (inspired by a Marwane Pallas photograph)

Interior art by Florin Cristea (Sculptures-Cristea Florin)

Text, cover and interior design by Crina-Ludmila Cristea

Copyright © 2019 Crina-Ludmila Cristea

All rights reserved

A Collection
of
MYSTERIES and DARK
TALES
of
IMAGINATION

In memory of

F. Scott Fitzgerald (1896-1940)

Margaret Millar (1915-1994)

Edgar Allan Poe (1809-1849)

Goran Stefanovski (1952-2018)

—

*To my mother and father,
and to Florin*

—

For helping me understand
this world, and myself,
a little bit better.
IT MATTERS.

CONTENTS

Author's Note........................8
Toward the Dark....................12
In the Forest of Bluebells........20
The Perfume Shop..................26
Stars and Snowflakes............34
Under the Apple Tree............46
Tender is the Rain.................51
The Hidden Chest.................56
Whispers............................63
Pricolici.............................72
In the Dream........................85
The Staircase.......................90
The Man in the Snow..............97
Acknowledgments..................103
About the Author...................104

Author's Note

Some of these stories were written a long time ago. One in particular (*In the Forest of Bluebells*) was initially written as a script (*Paint*) in my second year of university and has had several endings since the idea first came into my mind. Another one was conceived in the rush of imagination and is the seed that started a dark, psychological novel which is yet to be completed (*Tender is the Rain*). But most of the tales in this collection were written recently, as an experiment, while using the Reddit website and the nosleep community. That's how the bud of this collection sprouted.

The purpose of these stories was to scare the reader — *you* — and the basis was that they actually happened — they are true (even when they're not). They are written in the first person for this exact purpose.

It occurred to me, while putting together this note, that these stories are a small nod to the wonderful movies *Somewhere in Time* (1980), *The Last of the Mohicans* (1992), *The Crow* (1994), *Meet Joe Black* (1998), *What Dreams May Come* (1998), The *Butterfly Effect* (2004), *The Curious Case of*

Benjamin Button (2008), *Before Midnight* (2013), *Penny Dreadful* (2014-2016), and *Hemlock Grove (2013-2015)*. The books *Beast in View* (Margaret Millar), *The Catcher in the Rye* (J. D. Salinger), *In the Devil's Dreams* (Felix Blackwell), and many other stories, have also tremendously influenced my writing and fueled my imagination. I love all these masterpieces and they must have subconsciously impacted my life, as it often happens with great storytelling — it has an effect, it doesn't perish with time; it stays hidden and resurfaces when the moment is right. It shapes our lives, I think, and makes them better. I hope this book does the same for you.

I believe there is a world beyond this one — *perhaps more*. Some things can't be explained scientifically. Strange occurrences do happen, and sometimes — more often than not — they leave a trail of blood behind and traumatized individuals questioning their own existence. Real events have inspired these stories and made me eyeball the door and check out the shadows several times before falling asleep, so proceed carefully. Nightmares can trap you in their grip and might not let you go. You have been warned.
The darkness awaits you.

Toward the Dark

Deep, in the wretched and diseased claws of the city, lived a man. Not an ordinary man, but a man who could tell the future. I went to see him on a foggy night. I had been stuck here for a few weeks now — or they could be months, it's hard to keep track these days.

I was plummeting toward a dark void. That's the last I saw — that's *always* the last thing to see — a black sucking void. And the wind and the noise — they were *tearing* me *apart*.

I woke up dripping in sweat, hands trembling, nose bleeding. Body spent. Exhausted.

This morning the city was wrapped in a thick fog again — the skyscrapers nowhere to be seen. I hoped it to clear by midday, but it didn't. When the hours passed by and the damn fog still didn't clear, I began to worry more. I didn't want to go see him on a weather like this. Ghosts are lurking, always lurking. And they love the fog. The voices — they hide in it. Their screams have sharp fangs and reach me wherever I try to escape. So I do my best to keep out of their way, out of their territory. It doesn't always work out well. That's why I have to see this man. This visionary. *Seer of the future*, as he advertises himself. I have to do it tonight.

Despite the bleak weather, I am here, outside his door. The huge snake-head carved as his doorknob doesn't help out. But I have to knock. To enter his world. I have been running through nightmares for far too long. I crave the light. But it hardly comes nowadays. The last time I saw a proper sight of it was about 29 days ago. I took it for granted and now it was gone. Gone from my life. Maybe he can help me.

"You have to embrace the void," was the first thing he said to me. After I knocked on his door, using the creepy snake-head — shiny, cold and hard — he opened the door, but he didn't say a word — as if he knew I was coming, as if he was *expecting me*. He allowed me passage into his home and, with a sign of his hand, he encouraged me to sit on the chair.

I did, but after he said those words, I instantly wanted to leave. The conviction in his voice had me pinned to the chair, however. His cold and calculated voice stopped me. He knew *something*.

Terrified, but trying not to show it, I listened.

"Only in the dark you will find what you are looking for. What you are afraid of, you have to let go.

"You can go now. It will be better in your home. In your own comfort."

"But—"

"Go," he said. I frowned. The snake-look in his eyes told me all I needed: that was all the help he was willing to give me. All I would get from him tonight. *Go, or else,* his eyes said.

I stood up shaking, more from fear than frustration. I didn't want to go outside. I knew what was waiting for me. I didn't want to step out. But the man had already opened the door for me. I had to leave *his* home. But I also had to *stay alive*.

I turned back.

"Don't you even try," he said coldly, waving me off. "Just go ho—"

I threw a strong punch and knocked him off. He fell

on the hardwood floor, unconscious. I worried I hit him too hard, and was sorry for hurting him, but I didn't think I had other options left then.

"You fool, what have you done?" He said, licking his broken lip and spitting the blood from his mouth when he woke up.

"What I had to do."

I peered through his curtains at the creatures outside. One was just in front of his gate. Another one stood up on the old, broken wall, its eyes glowing fearlessly. They were scanning the area, looking for me. Another creature was on his doorstep, staring at the reptilian-carved doorknob. She was scratching with its long fingernail at the old polished wood. She was trying to enter. I shuddered and shut the curtains.

"What should I do? Tell me what to do."

"I've told you already. But you knocked me out instead. Fool." He shook his head disapprovingly.

"I need a place where I feel safe. I can't go out. Not now. Have you seen what's waiting for me?!"

"I know what's waiting for you. You have to *accept* it. Or you will *die*."

"You don't make any fucking sense, old man."

"You will understand. When the time comes."

I didn't know what that meant and the man refused to give me anything else. Frustrated and tired, I sat on the chair again, nervously shaking my right leg. I didn't know what to do. I was certain I was going to be slashed to pieces if I went outside.

I hadn't slept in a long time. I couldn't actually remember the last time I slept. Glowing eyes peered at me from the windows. Strong nails were scratching the glass, trying to break it — to get in. But the man had been smart: he had installed metal grates in his windows. I wondered — *I hoped* — that the creatures couldn't get in, and I fell into a deep sleep.

I woke up suddenly. My eyes, wide open in shock, peered around me in the dark. I couldn't move any of my limbs. I was paralyzed and falling again. But this time, it felt more like dying.

I tried to move my fingers, at least one of them, but none worked. It was like I had no motor functions anymore. Like I didn't run my own body. Like somebody else was controlling it, and *that somebody* wasn't doing a great job at that. I felt like dying, or something awful like that, but I didn't want to accept it. I was too young to die. I tried again to move. I slipped out slightly, and slipped back in again.

Not being in control was terrorizing. Horrifying. I was going to die, I was certain of it, despite my attempts to save myself. Something awful was going to happen.

Thousands upon thousands of thoughts crossed through my mind. I imagined falling into a cave full of snakes. They were going to consume me, bite their fangs into me and fill my body with their venom. I shook out of it and focused.

What had the man said? What did he say, what the fuck did he say...

That I have to accept it, or I will die. I glanced at the dark void piercing my eyes. I closed them and embraced the complete darkness. The wind tore at my skin, splitting it open. I could feel my bones breaking — bending — and crawling out of me. I could feel something *lifting*. It felt like *leaving*. It was disorientating and my head hurt. Pins and needles stung every inch of my forehead, every inch of my temples, and my back. And then, I lifted my head, pushed myself out completely, and opened my eyes.

I saw a man in the chair where I stood earlier. His head was bowed down. Wavy dark hair covered his crown. He seemed asleep. He looked like me. He looked *just like me*. He *was* me. I frowned. I saw the Seer of the future. He was next to the man — next to me.

I waved at him. To my surprise, he waved back and smiled. His lip, still smudged with blood, was swelling. He winced, licking the wound.

He stood up. He walked towards the man who was asleep on the chair — the man who looked very much like me. He was waiting patiently above him. What was he going to do to him — to *me*?

He looked for a moment longer, staring at the man's closed eyes — my eyes — then he walked away. He lit out a match and burned out some incense. Lavender, and sage.

The smell carried me further away. I was floating slightly better, but it felt like I was just about to fall off into a deep ocean, full of hungry sharks. I feared the creatures beneath, I feared the pain that awaited me after the fall. But somehow I found my balance. I was floating higher. The two men in the room were even further and distant now. I could see much more around me. It was strange, unfamiliar, but nonetheless fascinating. Creatures — no, wonderful beings were flying, buzzing around me in all directions. They were floating, like *long rainbow bubbles*. They looked *magnificent*.

I woke up suddenly. My body trembled and shook, as if electrified, for few more seconds. I was covered in sweat, but alive and back in the chair.

"Welcome back," the man said. "I see you didn't die, after all. Did you?" he said ironically.

"Here." He handed me a clean towel to wipe my face of sweat. I took it.

"It would have been more comfortable in your own home, in your bed, instead of this hard chair, but you didn't listen. Ah, well, it's all the same to me."

I stood silent, wiping my face, gathering my thoughts, and still shaking a bit. He passed me a cup of rose-hip tea and gave me a knowing nod.

"You have a mean punch. Don't do that again, or I'll have to hit you back. Okay?"

I sipped from the tea and nodded slowly.

"Tell me *everything* you know," I mumbled. "Please. I need to know."

"It all begins with the dreams. Or at least what we think are dreams. And the paralysis. To some, it takes longer than others. It took you 29 days, 21 hours and... 9 minutes, to be exact.

"You were on the other side of your body. *Out of it*, more exactly. But you know that. You *just* felt it."

"But...how...hmm...why...ahh..." I mumbled, looking for words. "Has it ever happened to you?"

"No, never to me. I seem to have a condition which does not allow me to dream. I don't remember them, anyway. But I see things, as you know. Not exactly into the future, as the pricey advert implies — that's just a trick — but into other planes of existence; into what other people see — experience. Into what *you* saw. You know now. It is not death what you feared. You just fell into something else entirely."

"I have always believed, more or less, in other worlds, in living other lives. *Past lives*. But *that*...I will never unsee that."

"Yes, it is quite something, *something good*, from what others have said, and what I can grasp from the visions I have, and from the spark that's back in your eyes," he said smiling. "Nobody can forget that. Most don't want to, anyway."

I nodded and sipped some more tea. I noticed there were no more creatures outside his windows, and the fog had cleared out. I could see the stars, despite the city light pollution.

Everything looked so different to me now. I sighed, relieved and eager to know more. To find answers. I had so many questions. I couldn't wait to float again. I just hoped next time I would be less freaked out of my own asleep body, and that getting out of it will be easier, less painful, and less frightening.

I knew what I was facing now — at least I had a clearer idea, and it wasn't death. It wasn't death *at all*.

Toward the Dark

In The Forest of Bluebells

I had been sitting at this table, drawing, for 3 weeks, almost every single day at lunchtime, until she took an interest in me and showed it. But lately, things were crumbling. Nothing was going as I had hoped. As I had expected. As they should have.

In those early days, she had her duties. She had to take orders, deliver food, scrape leftovers from the plates, emptying them into the bins. It was a busy restaurant and she was paid the minimum wage. So I was patient. And she always treated me kindly. Now, she didn't even look me in the eyes, and if she did, it was only to frown at me.
I drank some coffee left by her colleague on my table and turned my eyes to the drawing pad. I scribbled something, but I was not in the mood much. What was the point anymore?

A young couple entered noisily and sat at a table. They ordered food and then began to argue with each other as they were waiting.
I took another glance at her and sighed. She acted like I didn't exist. Probably, as far as she was concerned, there was no man sitting by the window, waiting for a modest smile from her — for a small sign that it wasn't all lost, that there was still some hope left. She was two tables away from mine and she didn't even glance at me. *Nope*, clearly, I didn't exist for her anymore.

I began to scribble. I got lost in it for a while. A few minutes later, I raised my head to look at the couple. They were giggling. She held a bouquet of lilies in her hands, sniffing them. Pleased, the young man smiled. I smiled too, and then turned the page with the happy couple and began to draw something else.

There was an old man, all cold and grumpy, at a table in the back corner. He shivered and pulled his scarf closer around his throat. He looked around, throwing menacing glances at the other customers and the waitresses. I drew a steaming cup of red bush tea in front of him. The old man poured some milk in, sniffed and smiled, and then he began to drink it, full of joy.

I gazed at her again. She continued to ignore me. I glanced at the happy couple and the happy man sipping tea and a thought occurred to me. I began to scribble again, this time a little more excited than before.

Waves crashed into the sandy shore and threw drops of salty, cold water on my skin. The sand was ticking the soles of my feet. The sun was golden, glowing on the calm sea in the distance.

A bell rang and the alarming noise shifted me from my reverie. Few plates with food were soon delivered to a table of four — two adults and two young kids, a boy and a girl. I glanced back at the couple. They were getting ready to leave. He had just paid their bill and she waited for him with a warm smile on her face, holding the lilies near. I gazed at them for a few more seconds, watching how they held hands and walked happily out of the restaurant. Through the window, I saw the kiss they shared and that gave me hope.

Back inside, the situation hadn't changed: she still didn't talk to me. After all the years and the memories we had together, I couldn't believe how easy it was for her to ignore me. I asked for another cup of coffee because I had finished my previous one, and because I hoped to get her to come to my table, but all she did was give me a frown in return. The old man drinking tea gave me a warm understanding look as if to say, 'I've been there before, boy, hang on tight'. I half smiled at him briefly, sighed, and started drawing again.

She was playing in the sand. Her wavy long hair moved quickly with the wind. She looked ahead at a white seagull that was walking on the seashore, scratching the wet sand, unafraid of the foamy waves rushing toward him.
I walked to her and took her in my arms. She stood up and we walked, hand in hand, across the shoreline. The fog was coming. She started to run away, giggling, and the seagull flew away too, high up into the sky, flapping his wings and flying with the wind. I looked at the writing in the sand. It said 'I love you'. The wind blew harsh sand into my eyes. I fell to my knees and blacked out.

I woke up in a tunnel — some sort of narrow chamber, surrounded by soil. I couldn't breathe. I couldn't find an exit. I was suffocating. I have always been terrified of tight, narrow spaces. But here worms crawled on the walls, on the floor, sliding on my bare feet. I could feel them bite into my skin as if I was already dead and rotting and they decided I was their perfect meal. I tried shaking them off, but they were stuck to me, like a wet black cold. They depended on me and they were not going to let me go. I pushed my fists into the wall, trying to break them. My fists bled and, as hard as I tried and fight it, I had barely damaged the walls. The darkness terrified me. I began sweating profusely. A rush of anxiety flooded over me. I had murderous thoughts. Suicidal thoughts. And then, in that complete darkness, with worms crawling all over my body, sucking from me, draining me of energy, of any hope of survival, I thought of her smile, sweet and gentle, like the song of a nightingale on a spring night. A bolt of warm light hit me.

I woke up laying down on the floor of a dark room, only lit by a few candles. But I could breathe better now, and I could even see a shape this time — a human shape: I was not alone. She was in the room as well. *My love*. But then I saw the knife with the long, sharp blade; it was right in-between us. A pain in my temples was killing me and I was still looking at my surroundings. I couldn't see much. Most of the room was cloaked in darkness like a velvet curtain had been pulled over it. It was eerily quiet. She began to wake up, and when she saw me, and the knife discarded on the floor, she rushed to grab it. The floor creaked as she moved hastily in the dim light to get the knife. I rushed too, but she reached it first and tried to slash me. She tried to cut me open twice this time and she did slit my shirt. Few lines of blood stained it. I didn't feel the pain yet, but I knew it was coming soon. She tried to cut me again, but I managed to grab her hand and shook the knife away. It fell with a loud thud on the wooden floor.

I embraced her and she accepted — she welcomed my touch and looked me in the eyes as if she recognized me — *she remembered me*. We began to kiss so we took over the small couch, making love.

Morning came. I woke up on a large white bed. See-through curtains filtered the warm, morning sun. I smiled at her, sleeping peacefully in my arms. I could hear giggles and robins chirping outside, in the bluebell forest. I stood up quietly and burned the remaining pages of the sketching notepad. I've put the ashes away and went back to join her in bed. But I held on to the pencil. I thought I hid it well. Maybe that was my (fatal) mistake. In fact, I know it was. Next time, if I do get another chance, I'll burn *everything*. I'll leave no traces, no opportunities, nothing that could separate us.

She is gone again. She found a way and sketched her own life. *A new life*. I am alone in the forest of bluebells now. No matter how hard I try, she escapes me. I wonder if I'll ever see her again. I wonder if I'll ever get her back, or if she'll forever forget who I am this time. I wonder if she'll find her way back to me. Maybe we are destined to be alone, never to find each other for too long. Maybe we are unfinished, messed-up drawings in someone else's life. Someone who knows better. Did we really think we had control? A way to love and be free? We are all puppets — *I* am just a puppet now. Forgotten, discarded. But not her, she can save us both.

Here, in the forest of bluebells, I wait for you. *Come back to me.*

In the Forest of Bluebells

The Perfume Shop

I was thirteen when my father decided to move us to another city. It was the same summer when I first met Miss Eve. She owned a perfume shop. She was, in fact, the most well-known perfumer in our area. Her hair was black as charcoal and had the most wonderful curls. Many wanted to find out what her perfumery secret was, but nobody ever did. Until one evening, when *I* decided to investigate.

Every now and then I think about her. And when I see her name, or one similar, in a novel or in a movie, the hairs stand up on my arms.

The way she looked that evening — it was breathtaking. She lifted a finger to her sensual mouth and silenced me — she pinned me with her eyes — I was frozen in place. I stood there, unable to make a move, and waited. Sweat began to form on my forehead. She got closer to me.

Remember this moment, a peculiar voice whispered in my ears. *In my head.*

Miss Eve put her hand on my forehead. Her eyes shone brightly — like two cold emeralds in the dark.

"Oh my, you're coming down with a cold," she said. "We better do something about it. *Fast.*"

She took me into the private, off-limits-kitchen of her perfume shop and made me a tea. Above anything else that one could have imagined to experience in such a place — roses, lavender, or vanilla beans — oddly, I could smell curry. The whole kitchen seemed infused with the smell of it. I looked for a large pot with the delicious, mouthwatering dish, but there was none in sight. She handed the tea and encouraged me to drink it. I sipped in silence, embarrassed and ashamed that I trespassed, and that instead of punishment, she took care of me.

She struck me as an old person, although she looked only about 35 years old. Even so, to someone like me, in those days, she looked like the mother I didn't have. The mother I wanted so badly. But it wasn't meant to be. I was to live an orphan, only with my father.

The police looked for her for months when she disappeared. People in the neighborhood put up posters — copies of hand-drawn sketches of her perfectly symmetrical face stared at me from shop windows, tree trunks, even car windshields. The whole neighborhood missed her, even the jealous wives. We all tried to find her. But we failed. She vanished. I never saw her again. Until today. I dipped my head from under the old, fancy gazebo and walked into the gallery, hand-in-hand with my partner, for an exhibition we had been invited at. We were greeted with champagne and red wine. My partner picked a glass with champagne, and I one with red wine. We began to mingle and observe our surroundings. And there she was, *staring* at me. She was pinned to the wall, *gazing* at me, in all her glory, from a massive oil portrait. There were many paintings displayed at the exhibition on that rainy evening, but that one took front stage. The frame was vintage and golden. It looked like it might have been made of gold. *Real gold.* I was mesmerized. She looked just like I had remembered her, even better somehow.

Come to me... someone whispered behind me. I turned and looked. There were a bunch of people gathered, having conversations about the art displayed and sipping red wine. But none looked back at me. My partner had wandered off with someone and was chatting with one of the artists. She left me on my own. *That was a mistake.* She should have known better, after all we've been through.

I turned back to the painting, dismissing the whisper and thinking it was probably just my tired mind playing some sort of trick on me. Or maybe the acoustics in the gallery were to blame, or something. Maybe I had too much red wine. Although I only had a half glass, I was always a poor drinker and only smelling the liquid often turned my eyes blurry and made my mind fuzzy. But that usually made me chatty, giggly, and a little bit flirtatious, I'll admit it. It didn't turn me into someone hearing strange voices, however. That never happened before, but I guess there's a first time for everything: hearing peculiar voices, kissing a woman, killing people... I brushed the strange thoughts away. I put the glass down on a silver tray and stood by, few meters away from the painting. There was an old chisel in display as well, inside a glass box nearby me. The wood handle looked broken in a few places, here and there, but the design carving on it — a small cat — still looked spectacular. The bent metal shone in the light. There was a faint but distinct smell of curry in the air. I thought someone forgot to shower before coming to the exhibition, and left it at that. But it made me hungry.

I looked back at the portrait, back into her eyes. The

woman stared at me intensely and while her eyes were painted pitch black, as were the rest of her features, I knew they were actually a different color. I hadn't seen them in years, but I could never forget them. Last time I looked into them, I saw death staring back at me. But the woman in the painting was now even more seductive, her gaze even more striking. It made me want to take my clothes off, then and there.

Damn wine, it had really gone to my head.

I brushed my left hand through my hair and undid my tie to turn down the heat in my body and to breathe better. She still stared at me, sending hot and cold urges down my spine. I looked for some water but there was none in sight. I fidgeted with my fingers and pretended to look busy, trying to appreciate the other artwork on display, but the painting called to me.

I straightened up and began walking towards it.

"Easy there, tiger." A feminine voice and a hand, lightly pressed onto my back, suddenly stopped me. "You've got the hots for the painted lady? You may want to be a bit more subtle..." My partner said, lowering her eyes to my bulge, hidden underneath my trousers, and then looked back at my face. She looked slightly amused, but still generally disappointed. I could always tell *that look* in her eyes. She was disgusted.

"Umm..." was all I could muster. Embarrassed, I covered my front with the umbrella I held in my hand. Thank God for the rain that night. I almost never carried one with me, but that evening, for some random, unknown reason, I decided I needed one. The rain hadn't even started, it wasn't even cloudy when we left our apartment, but somehow I knew it was going to pour. And it did.

"Excuse me," I said, and rushed to the bathroom.

I walked straight to the water basin and splashed cold water all over my heated face. Water droplets fell down my face. There was a cold in the air that I hadn't sensed when I entered. I noticed there was only one other guy in the bathroom with me. He was wearing newly polished shoes. His steps were echoing, drumming in my ears. I waited for him to leave.

"What do you want?" I whispered to the mirror.
No answer.
Feeling silly, I splashed some more cold water on my face and then started wiping it off.
I want you, I heard back.
I stopped instantly. Chills went up my spine.
I thought back to the beautiful woman depicted in the large portrait, hanging in the exhibition room nearby. My body, as if commanded by pressing a button, began rapidly to answer my thoughts. I could feel her on me...
But then I remembered the dead man from my childhood, blue and wrinkly in the bathtub filled to the top with a mixture of coarse salt, red crushed chilies, and some sort of oil — maybe coconut; he was like a sardine in a can — oily, crammed, and hidden from light — an experiment gone wrong in her kitchen. Or maybe an experiment gone perfectly right. Blood had stained the chunks of salt deep red. I looked for a sign of life — something — but his eyes were sewn shut; his lips too.
I want you... The voice whispered, and something — a tongue — licked my earlobe.
Give me what I want, the voice said, commanding yet seductive.
I undressed as quickly as I could. My naked body and face stared back at me from the large clean mirror.

A woman's face pushed slowly through it.

I gasped. She was more beautiful than ever before. She had not aged a bit. In fact, she looked slightly younger.

She wrapped her delicate, soft hands around my neck and began touching my face with hers.

Exactly at that time my partner entered. The shock and rage on her face were more than enough. I knew she was going to leave me. She had put up with plenty from me. The sleepwalking, the masturbating, the nightmares, now the naked public display — of course she had enough. She walked off, wiping tears off her face, without saying a single word.

I turned to the mirror unperturbed.

The woman pulled me closer toward her, grabbed me, making me hers. No longer a boy this time, but a man. I felt used in her hands — dirty — but I enjoyed it. Then, I felt a thick liquid dripping down my cheek, down my jaw, my neck. Drops of blood dripped on the floor, *one by one*, faster and faster.

Bloooood mirrror...rrr...

A sharp, excruciating pain hit me and I fell to the cold floor of the sparkling clean bathroom.

Minutes later, a 30-year-old man walked in and found me with a chisel stuck into my head, rapidly losing blood. The thick, warm liquid had dripped down my face and painted my cheeks like a ritual mask brought back from the old ages. The man shrieked. I heard him push himself back into the wall and bumping into the door, trying to exit, maybe to get some medical assistance, or some sort of help. Or just to run. But the door would not open. Did not open.

Cooome to meeee... I heard again, whispered

faintly.

A dark tall shape, cloaked in darkness, moved slowly towards the terrified man, who covered his face with his hands, shook from all his limbs, and tried to scream. But his mouth no longer said anything. His vocal cords had stopped working properly.

My blood covered most of the bathroom floor — *a blood mirror now* — and the man fell down, squirming in it. He made monstrous noises, but not one single clear word was let out from his contorted mouth.

I smiled at the woman in the mirror.

Then, the man vanished, consumed by the blood. *By her.*

Soooo beauutiiifuuuuul...

She gently took my hand in hers. I kissed her, savoring every single pore, *her perfume, her touch*, and joined the other men standing heads-bent at her feet. We were more then. We are more *now*.

The Perfume Shop

Stars and Snowflakes

It was 5 am when I heard the scream. I opened my eyes wide and stood up. Listened carefully. Maybe I had imagined it. Misheard it. The fire in my fireplace had gone cold few hours ago, but my room was still warm, despite the long winding crack in the wall. *I have to get on and fix that one day. Before it gets bigger and brings the whole house crumbling down.*

I turned back towards the window, listening.

And then it came again, loud and horrifying, like it was escaping the bowls of Hell.

Shaking, I stepped out from the bed in my pajamas and went at the window. The snow had covered the edges of the frame and the glass was encased with thin ice. The visibility was severely reduced. It was still pitch black outside, except for a light at the end of the yard. I inspected the area, as much as I could, given my restrictions, but I couldn't see anything suspicious. There were a few cars, mostly covered in snow as well, on the street near my house, but otherwise everything was...normal. It was an ordinary January morning.

Heeelp!

I shook. I couldn't place where the scream was coming from and that worried me further. *Someone needed help.* But who? And where?

I quickly put on my trousers and a thick flannel and searched through my mind. What could it be...where it was coming from...why it sounded so pained, so distant, yet so strong.

I had watched a documentary a few months ago

about the serial killer Ted Bundy, and other videos about different kind of killers and how they would strike. One of the things that really stood out to me was one case. One time, a man attacked a woman — a young college student — near her apartment block. A neighbor heard her screams and apparently he yelled and spook the attacker away. He had stabbed the woman, but ran away. It was nighttime. The woman managed to enter her apartment block, bleeding, but still alive. Moments later, however, the attacker came back and stabbed the woman 56 times. She screamed for help, but nobody came out. That information shook me to the core. *A woman laying bleeding on a cold floor, being overpowered and repeatedly stabbed by a man, within reach and safety of her apartment, yet she was to suffer a painful, brutal death.* I wondered where was the neighbor who had initially yelled at the attacker, scaring him away. Had he not called the police, checked if the woman was fine the first time she was attacked? But mostly, I wondered where the other neighbors were and how come nobody came out to help the poor woman while she was screaming and struggling to defend herself for more than 45 minutes. All that awful time and nobody came out to her rescue. She could have been saved. Instead, she *bled* to death, in excruciating pain, probably thinking nobody cared about her.

It was a primal scream, for survival, what I heard.

I was not going to be that kind of neighbor. I was not going to lay awake in my bed waiting for the screaming to stop. I had to do something. I grabbed my phone and quickly called the police. After I gave them my address, I waited as per instructed by the policewoman. But then the screaming started again. I decided there was no time to spare. I pulled a jacket over and ventured outside in the bitter cold. I could hear the screaming better then, more clearly. It was coming from the large oak tree. There was a dark trail leading towards the trunk of the tree. I looked carefully and realized it was blood. I looked at the tree in the distance and scanned the area quickly. The screaming had stopped. *Ceased completely.*

Shit, I thought. *I should have waited for the police. Someone very dangerous, very vile, could be behind that tree. Someone stronger than me.*

That's why those neighbors hadn't come out to help that woman — they were scared for their own lives. *But I had to play the hero. Idiot.*

I stepped slowly towards the tree, my eyes sharp, despite the sleep still lingering on my eyelids.

I walked around the tree, from a distance, not getting too close to it. I looked at the snowed ground expecting to see a body. Blood, human flesh, dismembered limbs — there was nothing of the such behind the tree. No track of a struggle, no body. I frowned, more shocked at that discovery than anything else. It didn't make sense. I had seen the trail of blood leading there but that had suddenly ended near the trunk, just half a meter or so away from it. The snow there was completely white. There was no drop of blood, nothing at all that could point to a savage attack.

There were several tracks in the snow but from the size of them I assumed they were from squirrels. Except it had snowed overnight. I doubted squirrels were up so early.

And then a mouth shouted right in front of my face, so loud and so sudden it had appeared that it made me lose my balance and stumble to the ground. I fell and hit my head on the tree trunk. Everything went black.

As far as I can remember, I was always fascinated with movie stars which is why I wasn't startled when I saw Marilyn Monroe in front of me, dressed in a white, sparkling gown, like a perfect sculpture — a deity in the snow. She looked real and I didn't question it because I had imagined her in front of me, on top of me, behind me, wrapping her arms around my neck — I had imagined her many times to satisfy myself. Her and many others. But I felt something sticky and when my hand touched the back of my head and come up with dirty red fingers, I knew something was awfully wrong. I just wasn't sure what. I couldn't remember why I was outside, in this sharp stinging cold.

Suddenly, Marilyn Monroe took my hand and led me away. I followed, mesmerized, as if in a dream.

We reached an illuminated building — a bar, one could say. It was in the middle of nowhere. I didn't remember being there before, but I followed anyway.

There was a figure of a man standing in the dark, leaning by a wall. He looked eerily familiar. His long, black wavy hair blew in the wind. He stood lonely and a sudden urge to speak with him came over me, but Marilyn pulled me away.

Let him be, she seemed to say. *He's got demons to wrestle with. Let him be.*

A crow landed on his shoulder and he looked at her but said nothing, as if he'd taken a vow of silence.

Marilyn pulled me close and we went in. My old clothes had suddenly vanished and they were replaced by an elegant suit. I checked my breast pocket. There was a purple handkerchief tucked in. *Nice*.

H.C. — one of the greatest characters ever created in American literature — was by the bar, standing right next to his creator, Mr. S. He was telling him something about the ducks and how they froze in time. How nobody found them, but that they're still alive, somewhere, little ice statues. I gazed at the duo, fascinated by their conversation and by how one was young and the other old in appearance, yet they both seemed much younger, as if a child — *the same child* — possessed them both, but not in a bad way. They seemed alive, *free*.

I looked around. The room was full with dancing girls and there was a mime somewhere further away from the bar. He was showing off, the crowd was cheering.

To my left there was a lift and to my right was a stage. In the center of it was a staircase. It glimmered as if it was made of diamonds. Marilyn laid on it bare. Her white skin seemed to glow, to take over the whole room.

I shivered.

Why am I still cold? I wondered. *Everyone seems to be comfortable and warm in here, dancing and giggling and having a great time, in general.*

"You are still alive, my friend, that's why. If I were you, I'd worry if I didn't feel the cold anymore," said Mr. F. Scott Fitzgerald, (looking just like that famous movie star who played him, Tom... something.) I stared at him, unsure what he meant by that. He patted me on the back and gave me a fancy glass of something — I think it was spicy gin — but, unfortunately, I had to refuse him. I don't drink alcohol, you see. It makes me sick. The smell of gin especially, even just a few whiffs of it, gives me headaches. I prefer tea, but I doubted they were gonna give me that in there if I asked. Fitzgerald held the glass from the stem and sipped from it, staring curiously at my face. I had so many questions to ask him and I was just about to do it, when a girl wearing only a thin, sky-blue dress, who looked exactly like my first sweetheart from high-school — long blond curls bouncing on her back and shoulders, clear blue eyes, rosy full lips — asked me in a French accent if I wanted to dance. She saw me hesitate, so she grabbed my arms and pulled me to the dance floor. We engaged in a close dance. I was rather taken with her. Our bodies seemed to mold together as one — *we were so close.* We were just about to kiss when Marilyn suddenly turned up, too. She looked more glamorous than ever before. Alive. Happy.

She raised her perfectly shaped eyebrows at me, making me aware of something — *someone.*
You wanted to speak with him. Try now.

I looked at the tall man and his face painted black and white. The crow sat on his left shoulder. He held his face in long strong palms. I sat down beside him.
"It's nice to listen to the rain sometimes, I get it. I like to listen to it when I'm sad."
He looked at me, frowning, but said nothing.
It wasn't actually raining, but it felt suitable to say that to him. I always loved him in that movie. It was such a tragedy it was his last.
"Hey, shouldn't you be somewhere else by now, with someone you love deeply? What are you doing

here on your own, lonely? You're not that kind of man."

He gazed at me with his dark, olive-green eyes. They lit with apprehension. He smiled and stood up. He threw his black cape dramatically, but somehow he made the move look cool.

The tall man caressed the black bird on the head and brought it close to his heart.

The crow started shedding its black feathers and in their place white ones started sprouting out. In fact, the entire bone structure of the bird had changed — the crow was no longer a crow, but a dove. The man's entire face was bright now. *Illuminated.* He stretched his arm before him and raised his palm. The dove stepped gently on it and turned into a small woman, growing gradually. The lean man took her into his arms and kissed her. They kissed with the kind of love one only finds once in a lifetime, and then, together, flew away into the light. I could hear boisterous distant laughs. I smiled. Tears fell quietly down my face.

H.C. and Mr. S. patted me on the back.

"Let's find the ducks," I said. "I don't know how to swim, but somebody has to save them. Tell them they're not forgotten. Someone cares."

They both nodded and I though I could see tears starting to form in their eyes as well.

But then, the woman in the blue dress grabbed my hand again. She wanted to dance once again. I politely declined.

"I have to go and find them, make sure they're ok."

That scream — it started again. It came from the bathroom now. I rushed there and in my haste I didn't notice the people in the vicinity *turning* until later. They were all staring at me. Their faces had aged and they looked more dead than alive. They reached to grab me. One stumbled into a stool and crashed face down onto the floor. Few bones broke and fell scattered at my feet. I stumbled back. The rest of them were still coming towards me strong. The mime was trying to hit me with a baton and the dancing girls were bare bones now. The elegant clothes hung lose on their ashen bones and they clanked towards me on their high-heels, as if engaged in a macabre dance.

One more dance, one of them hissed. *One more dance,* another shouted.

I ran to the bathroom as fast as I could and locked the door behind me.

"Who are you?" A young voice said softly just behind me.

I turned carefully.

A little girl sat down leaning by the cold wall.

She looked alive and familiar, but I didn't know why or where I knew her from. Maybe her blond curls reminded me of a friend I had, or maybe it was her eyes. They were sad.

"What are you doing here, alone in the night?"

"I am always alone," she said.

I sat down beside her and caught my breath momentarily. The zombies, or whatever they were, could wait a few moments. There was always time to spare for a conversation with a kin soul.

"Where are you from?"

"Oh, just over from the riverside. I have a place there. I mean… I had."

"Oh?"

"The storm tore it apart. They aren't there anymore."

"Your parents?"

She nodded and started sobbing.

Loud banging began at the door. They were close, the old, broken creatures.

"Hey, *hey*, give me your hand. We have to leave this place. Come."

We stood up. I checked the window. It was opened. It looked large enough for a child to escape. I raised the girl on my shoulders and she got through.

Just then, the zombies — or whatever kind of creatures they were — broke the door and filled the bathroom. They looked hungry. I scrambled through my mind and thought about The Walking Dead. I couldn't remember an episode in which the characters escaped from a bathroom filled with zombies ready to devour them. But I hadn't watched all the episodes, so I could be wrong, maybe there was someone who had gone through that. Maybe there was a way, maybe someone had escaped from something like this. Maybe they survived. *Yeah, right.* If only I was that lucky. But I was no movie star and the bathroom was clearly not a movie set. I didn't have a script, I didn't know what was going to happen next.

"Come," the little girl said, but it was too late for me. One exit was blocked by the creatures and the other one looked way too small for me to fit through. But I did not intend to die there.

I looked in the mirror.

"Save me. Just this once."

A bunch of heavy snow fell on top of my head and pushed me to the ground.

What the hell? Where the heck am I?

I looked around, relieved that somehow I had

escaped the morbid creatures, but confused. It was dark and I didn't know where I was, but when I looked up, I saw the top of the large cherry tree and the little tree house I built when I was a kid. It was still standing, after all these years.

Surprised and a little lightheaded, I stood up.

I could see my grandfather's house in close distance. A wave of relief washed over me. A light was on in his kitchen. I looked around but there was nobody. Only a few small tracks in the snow, leading back to the house. They looked like a child's soles. I brushed the snow off my palms and followed the tracks, but they had disappeared when I reached my door.

I'll see you again sometime, someone whispered closely in my ear. Then, I heard a giggle, faraway in the wind, and it started to snow again. I went in, lit a fire and started to boil a large pot of water to make some chamomile tea. My head still hurt, I had to make sure I treated the wound and cleaned away any infection I could have, internally or externally.

"Up so early?" my grandfather said, surprised, from outside my window.

"Why not?" I said, smiling.

"Why not, indeed," he replied cheerfully. "Maybe you're feeling like cleaning the pathway later. Looks like there's going to be a lot more snow today."

"You can count on me," I replied. He walked back to his kitchen.

Light from the embers in the fireplace painted the cracked wall in warm tones. *I really have to get on and fix that crack one day soon, before it brings the whole house crumbling down.* I wonder if it can be done though. Some which are broken can never be fixed, not usually. I turned back towards the window, listening and sipping my tea. Snow was falling.

A police car stopped at the gate, blasting its bright colorful lights onto the sparkling snowflakes.

Shit, I forgot I called them. I guess I'll have some explaining to do. But it will all be ok, I know it will.

I sipped a bit more tea and then walked outside, letting the snowflakes caress my body, like I was on a movie set, just about to shoot a scene. *Ready.*

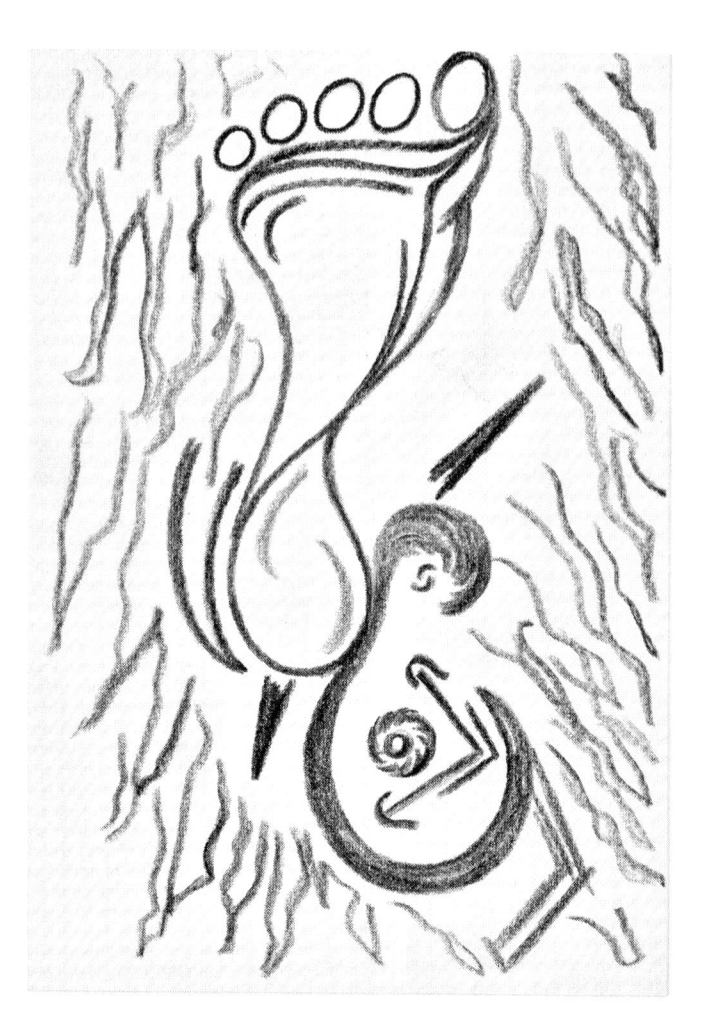

Stars and Snowflakes

Under the Apple Tree

There are very few things I'm scared of in this life. Unlike other people, I am not scared at the sight of spiders — no matter how large they might be; I am not scared of pigeons or other birds plucking my eyes and eating them like in a Hitchcock movie (at least, I don't give much thought to that kind of stuff you see in horror movies). I am not scared of flying in an airplane, or of heights. I am not scared of running into a burning building. Somehow — I don't know how or why — I am not scared of dying. (I am only scared of the pain which I assume comes just before the passing.) I do, however, have two great fears that often haunt my dreams:

I am afraid of someone hating (me) intensely, and expressing that hate;

I am afraid of someone physically and verbally abusing me. It makes me shake, it makes me sick.

When my grandmother died I was 4.

I remember sitting in the back of the truck, by her dead body, and wondering why all those people were crying and following us.

She was dead. I knew that and I understood there was some ritual to be taken care of, to take her on her last ride.

My cousin was in the truck with me as well. She was younger than me and cried a lot — I remember briefly her runny nose and her small hands — her face contorted by the realization that something other than life exists and is here to take the ones she loves. Nothing was going to be the same again. Her joyous countenance saw a piece of her break that day, chipping and scratching at her insides.

My grandmother's skin was covered in spots of sickly yellow and purple. Her feet were swollen, the veins in her legs were clogged with blood, and I could see the purple-black outlines bulging out, almost coming out of her, crawling out.

She never liked me. She hated me in fact; or maybe she hated my mother, therefore, she hated what my mother created. *Me.*

After we laid her to her eternal sleep in the ground, we came home. I imagine we had tables set up in the yard and people from the village came to have wine and stuffed vine leaves, to honor her and say their goodbyes. (This is the usual ritual for honoring the dead in my country.) But I don't remember that taking place. As I mentioned already, I was only 4. I don't remember much now, 24 or so years later.

Days after her burial I was certain that the room in which her body lay that last day was haunted. I was almost certain she was still inside there, waiting to catch me and give me a beating if I dared to enter. I still remember her hands bound in silent prayer, her feet tied together as if not to go running and haunting the living.

She was clearly dead. Worms probably crawled on her body and ate from it by now. But this didn't stop me — I avoided that room in which I last saw her like the plague. After her death and her burial, I often walked on the cracked cement alley, which leads from my grandfather's kitchen to the gate and the road, to go and visit my older cousin. But as soon as I got near that part of the house with *that* room — from which I felt she was watching me — I would swerve a large half circle in front of it and run towards the gate, pulling it hard, to open it as fast as possible, and ran away from whomever could be following me — whoever could be trying to grab me. *To catch me.*

You see, me and my grandmother, we used to play a game: I would hide and she would try to find me. You may think this was cute if it wasn't for the fact that she was looking to give me a beating equal to death.
I don't know why she hated me so much.
I don't know why I think she did.
After all, I only remember her hitting me only in one instance. But I remember hiding from her behind an apple tree in my cousin's yard and praying to God not to let her find me. My heart beat fast, almost bursting from my chest. I looked at the yellow apples and held tight to the tree trunk.
*Please don't let her find me, please...*I prayed and prayed. The moment only lasted a few seconds, maybe minutes at most. She walked in the yard and chatted to my grandfather's sister. She asked where I was.
I shot up from under the yellow apple tree, with its grand panoply of thick green leaves, and rushed through the cracked gate. The wood squealed when I pushed it, and she heard me then. I ran as fast as I could, but her wooden whip still caught my legs and part of my bottom. They turned red instantly. I shrieked and burst into tears, more from fear than pain. *She bruised me.* She haunted me on the road as I ran back home, calling me names I will not repeat here, names which no young child should hear, or have had been their target.

She is dead now and, while I feel sorry for my father's pain — his loss — I am relieved and I breathe a little bit freer. But even now, after all these years, when I go to visit my grandfather, I still remember those dark days when my grandmother's ghost haunted me. And I fear she might still be in that room, still waiting. I almost jump off the cement alley to step on the grass. I almost half-circle the front of the building to avoid locking eyes with the ghost of a woman with an iron grip. And then I remember: I'm older now and I don't believe in ghosts.

Behind the yellow stained curtains and the dust-covered glass, I think I see a face with gray hair, black-purplish hands, and I imagine her thick swollen feet running towards me. I rush to the gate and close it behind me. I embrace my grandfather, kiss him on the cheek, and tell him I'm in a hurry to catch the bus.

Because ghosts don't exist. And ghosts don't come crawling out from the past without asking for permission, like the gray-haired one, waving from the window behind my grandfather's kind face, turning her goodbyes into a fist and clenching her teeth, crunching them at me, snapping and twisting each bone in her undead body.

Ghosts don't exist. *Not like this one.*

Under the Apple Tree

Tender is the Rain

Heavy raindrops were falling on the roof, hitting the window. The almost nude trees were fighting the storm. They clearly did not want to become wreckage. A few rusty leaves were still clinging by the wet roof window, still battling to look alive. They were not alive really, not anymore. I looked at the woman. My face was right in front of her face, my eyes looking straight into her eyes. We smiled at each other.

I removed her clothes slowly, taking all of her in. I washed her with my bare hands. She felt so protected. She loved the fresh smell of blueberries the soap left on her skin. I loved it too. I always did. After I dried her with a white soft towel, she noticed I was hard and smiled seductively. She took my hand in hers and led it to her breasts, caressing them all over, gripping them. I closed my eyes. My heart was pumping. I was so hard I thought I will explode. She got closer and moved my hand down her naked belly to feel her. Her nipples got hard and her hand led mine even lower. Then and there I gripped her and touched it all over. I've put my hand on it firmly, and then, between her legs, I reached her bottom. I grabbed it hard and pulled her in. She was still a little bit wet from the bath. I squeezed my finger inside her, first tempting her, playing with her, wetting her more and more, and then, in a quick move, I led myself all the way inside her. She screamed of pleasure, drops of sweat down her breasts and belly mingled with the wetness between her legs. She squeezed her breasts and bit her lower lip until it turned rosy. She admired my strong arms and caressed them. She went down, gently touching my naked abdomen with her nude breasts. This was heaven. She went even lower. She wanted to take me in her mouth but I refused. She didn't know what else to do with me because she was enjoying it so much. I didn't give her much time anyway. I slipped two of my fingers in her again, reaching that spot quickly, and she screamed again. This time I was harder on her. She liked that too. It gave me great pleasure.

I gazed at the window and listened. The storm outside was in full spectacle. It gave everything it had. Thunders, lightning, rain, heavy drops of rain. *Fresh rain.* The trees still seemed to fight, though. They would not cease this battle easily. Branches kept on wrestling with the wind, they fought even at the cost of losing their last rusty leaves. It was a battle of life and death. They did not want to be murdered. They wanted to survive. I wondered if they will. I smiled. I always liked the rain, the storm. It calmed me down. I turned my face from the wet window back to the pleasured wet body. I gazed at it almost satisfied. I gently touched her cheek and kissed it. Her skin was so soft. She was so delicate, almost like a flower. Like a flower in the storm. I closed my eyes and breathed in her perfume. When I opened my eyes everything turned into an awful splash of red. I looked again at the woman, laying on the cold surface. This time she was not enjoying it. She was almost lifeless. She looked at me terrified. She was still conscious. Barely. Seconds earlier she was experiencing a great deal of pleasure. A great deal of pleasure. Now she was laying on the bathroom floor, her neck and breasts painting the white tiles a vivid red. She looked me deep in the eyes whilst giving her last performance. Her big eyes with her long eyelashes were fixated on me. Perhaps she wanted to know why. They all showed that painful desire to know. *Why? Why was that happening to them?* They would never find out.

She gave her last breath while I was still painting her portrait. A pool of red liquid painted the bathroom floor which was now turning into a darker red color, like ripe cherries. On a canvas that earlier was empty, a figure was now taking shape. I smiled. I brushed the last missing lines within the red foggy background. The figure within the painting felt so alive. So inspiring, but mostly so alive. I inhaled the perfume of fresh paint and put the brush down. I gazed back at the still body. She was even more beautiful now. So still, yet so alive. I wondered if I will miss her voice. Her screams of pleasure. Perhaps I will.

Later that night, I carried her body to the river. She would be the only one whose body was never found. The dirty river took her away and she was never seen again. *I* never saw her again. If her body was ever found, I doubt her identity had been revealed. She was probably food for the fish in the ocean. By now, she had already been consumed, her particles dissipated in the water, the mud, the air. I missed touching her sometimes, but like her there were many others. I could replace her, of course I could, and I did, but I never forgot her. I never forgot any of them. I kept on listening to the rain instead.

In the close distance of my house, I saw a tree

struck by lightning. I smelled the fresh smoke coming from the tree. Large drops of rain kept falling on my face, all over my skin, caressing it. I smiled, satisfied, and kept on walking on the cobbled streets with the yellow light of the lamps reflected on their wetness. I never forgot any of them. I kept on listening to the rain instead. It calmed me down.

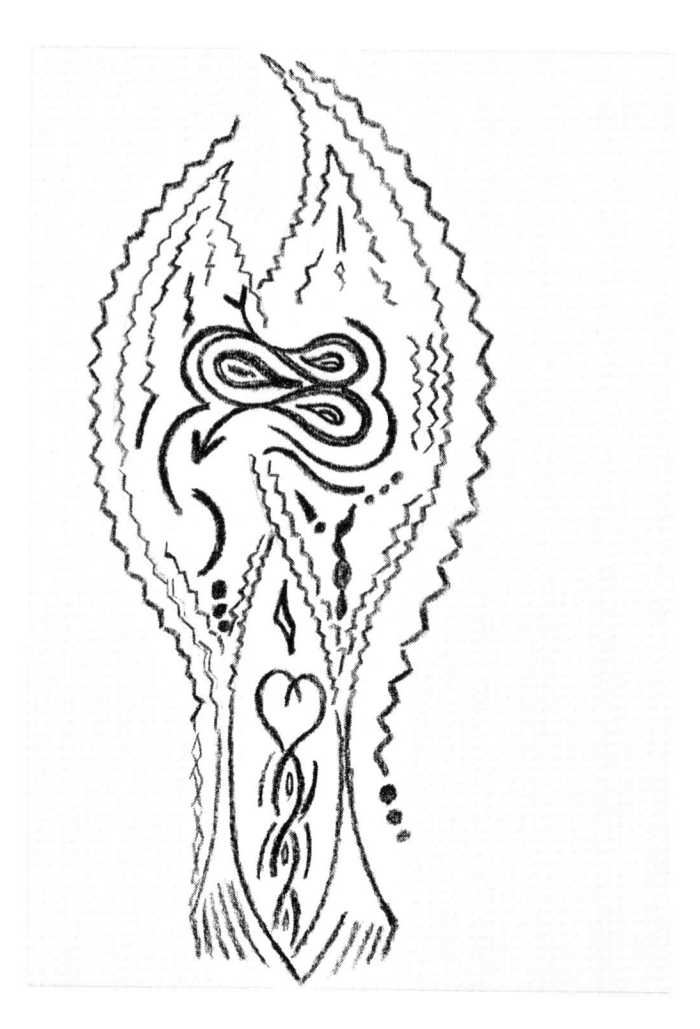

Tender is the Rain

The Hidden Chest

That summer the heat was unbearable. I took my notebook and pencil of choice and went to the barn.

The barn was at the back of the garden. I had been sitting in there for a good hour or so when, accidentally, I stumbled upon a crack in the old wooden floor. I reached to put the wood back in place, but when I looked through the crack I saw more than darkness. There was an old chest covered in dust and spiders. I wondered what could be in it. I knew the estate had once belonged to a writer, one of the most famous writers in the world. In his late years, according to the media, he had become a recluse — an awful word to use for any kind of artist, or human being, in my opinion.

I wondered if the chest was full with manuscripts, stories that have not seen the light of publication. My fingers trembled with anticipation at the thought of that. Unseen manuscripts — there was magic in that. Although I was a playful painter and aspired to be an illustrator, I had always been fascinated with stories and the written word.

I looked at the floor to see if a latch was somewhere hidden. There was nothing of the sort in sight. While I broke the old floor bit by bit, careful not to fall through the wood bitten by the jaws of time, I wondered how the chest had been put in there. The only logical options seemed to be that either there was a different entrance, accessible from another part of the barn, or the chest had been put in there before the floor was installed. As I worked at the wood, a splinter went through my skin and stung my thumb. I stopped to remove the old cracked wood and to wipe the dust away from my skin. A few drops of my blood colored the floor and one fell down onto the chest. A loud noise came out from the dark hole. I heard a loud snap, as if a lock had been broken, or more like unlocked. I stumbled back, startled by the noise. Then a whisper came out and a cold wind brushed my cheek, which in the awful stifling afternoon air wasn't all that bad. But the whisper terrified me. What was buried in there? A human being? An animal? I expected (and secretly hoped for) pages yellowed by time, not weird noises. I liked drawing creatures, not facing them. I stood up to leave, with the thought in mind to return with a friend or two, maybe even an adult, but another whisper stopped me.

"I have something for you," it said.

I stood back, listening.

"Aren't you even curious to find out what it is? Come, boy, *come closer.*"

I got closer and since the voice stopped, I took the drawings and the stories out. *There is a reason why he buried them,* I thought. *He never wanted them published. Maybe he wanted to rebel against publishers, back in his time. Maybe that's why he buried them in this old chest and hid them from light, from anyone.* The truth was another, but I couldn't have known then. He became consumed by a creature he created. It came hunting him, both during the day and the night. He had no more peace anymore. He buried the manuscripts hoping to get rid of it. And years later, I had found them. As a lover of stories and old tangible things, I had found a treasure better than gold, or any precious gem stones. It was knowledge nobody else had.

The curiosity got the better of me. I took the manuscripts out carefully, one by one, dusting them out, attentive not to break the fragile pages. The dust lifted off and I could read them.

I could read them all right now, I thought. *Such a treasure. Such a gift.*

"Give us more of your blood," the voice whispered suddenly. "In exchange, we will make you rich. What do you say?"
"My blood?" I mumbled, terrified. "What do you need my blood for?! What do you want to do with it?"
"Just write another story," the voice said.
I frowned and ran away.

Thinking back on that day, I am so proud of that kid. He ran away, but he didn't get himself in trouble. I ran then, like a coward. *I should have kept running.*

Years later, when I was in my early twenties, I returned to the barn.
My grandfather was dying. I came to say goodbye. As I tried to find a quiet time and a place to sit after his passing, I retreated to the back of the garden. We used to pick strawberries there, on the long pathway leading to the barn. They were the ripest and sweetest I have ever tasted in my entire life. I laid on the grass and listened to the chirping of birds and thought about the face of my old man. I would never see him again. I was terrified the memory of his face was going to slip through my mind and get lost within dark corners. What got him was bound to get me as well, sooner or later.

Suddenly, as I was laying on the grass, I heard a hoarse voice. *Old and sick.* It was coming from the barn. I wondered if anyone got lost. I thought maybe a friend of my grandfather or... who knows and who cares what I thought in that moment — I was wrong, that's all that matters. *No one was lost there, except me, maybe. The voice I heard, it knew exactly where it was. Where it lived. That voice never got lost. Only trapped. And I released it.*

You have to understand, years have passed and I had forgotten all about the voice I heard when I was just a boy. So I didn't suspect a thing. I wasn't afraid. I was just...never mind. If only I had remembered, maybe I could have avoided all this mess.

Anyway, I walked in the barn. I found the hidden chest again. The voice was coming from inside of it.

I took the pages out and read the story the writer made up decades ago probably.

I started drawing the creature. I didn't know then, but with every line I drew, I become his slave — a painter at his command. I made him real. *I made the monster real.*

He promised to make me rich. I was struggling, I barely had enough money to cover my bills and food. There were days when I feared I would end up on the streets. So when the request came again, all those years later, I thought about it and didn't think it could do any harm. *Five drops of my blood on the manuscripts hidden in the chest. What could go wrong?* I thought. *In the worse case scenario, I'll lose a minute amount of blood. In the best case scenario...*

He made me famous. I was a proper grown up,

living a grown up life in a large, comfortable house, but I couldn't care less. Nothing tasted like before. I couldn't find pleasure in anything. The only thing I was doing all the time was paint. *Paint, paint, paint.* That was all I did, most of the time. It was always on my mind.

I began to have terrible nightmares. Only they weren't nightmares. Creatures started to hunt my dreams demanding to be made. *Freed.* Every night and every moment I closed my eyes to rest, they came. I wished them away, but it was futile. The more I asked them to leave me alone, the more they came at me. Until one night, when I woke up sweating and staring into their glistening eyes. They stood just above me, with heavy feet on my bed, on my chest, whispering.

According to the media, I had gone mad.

There was a stinging itch, a throbbing pain in my thumb. I feared it was infected, but I didn't know from what. I checked with the doctor and found nothing. I thought maybe I was going crazy, maybe my grandfather's illness caught up to me sooner than expected.

I did everything in my power to get rid of the pain, of the nightmares. I even cut my thumb, removed it from my hand completely. But I think I did it too late. It was in my blood, in my brain. It can't be removed unless I die, and even that is questionable. Will they go away when I'll die? *I'm not so sure.*

You stare at me incredulously, detective, but I'm telling you: I didn't do it. I didn't kill anyone. I mean I did, but *I didn't*. Do you understand what I'm saying?

They made me do it. They have a plan, and I was only their instrument in executing part of it. I am not the architect, you must believe me.

    For all the pain, there is a story, detective. I wonder if mine will be remembered. But I know better. And I don't expect forgiveness because I don't deserve it. I have caused pain. Of my own accord or not, the fact remains that I have hurt people. I just want you and the ones left behind to understand why. To make sense of this all. To make sure it doesn't happen again. Because they do plan to do it again, trust me. Especially now, when there's more of them. They won't stop. Not until we're all *dead*.

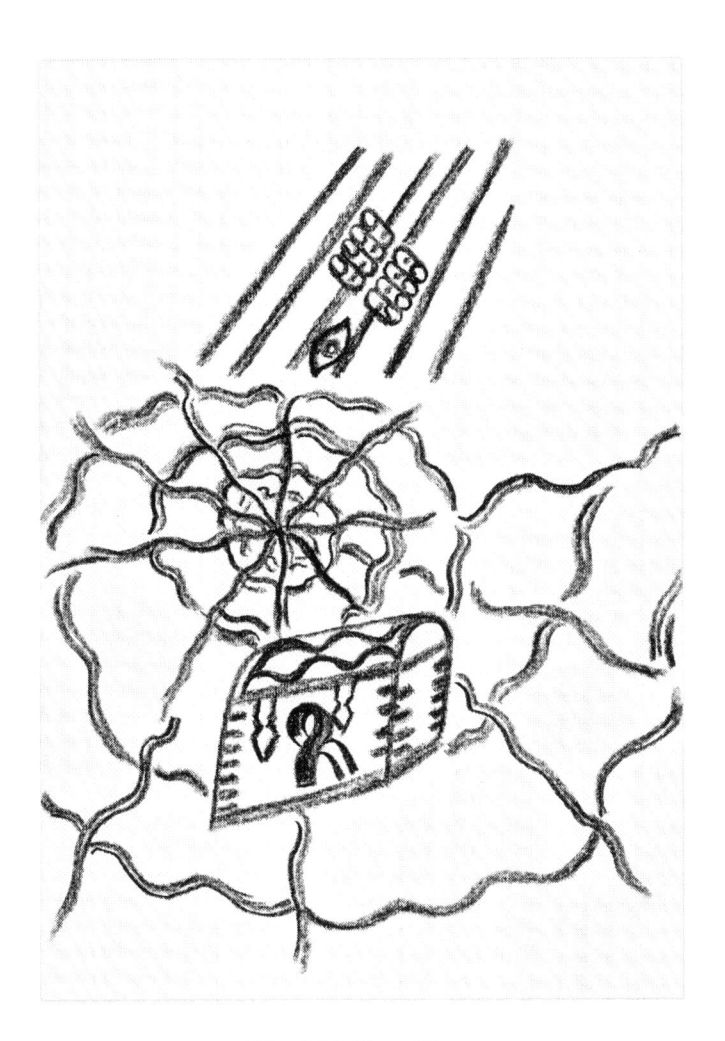

The Hidden Chest

Whispers

I fell asleep on an odd tree trunk and woke up on the other side.

This all began when I rose up in the middle of the night to take a piss. By then, I had been living in the woods for 6 months. I had seen several deer, a brown bear, and a wolf. But what I saw that night changed my entire perception of the world again.

What is real, what is not — I don't know anymore. My eyes scanned their bodies to make sure they were real. Thirteen women, of various ages, laid asleep by the trees nearby my yurt, inside the circle of stones. One of them even sang in her sleep. I was still not sure if I was imagining them or not, so when they didn't answer my call, I touched the ankle of the one in the middle. The smooth skin was warm. The bones underneath it were strong. One of them yawned and startled me, but then gone back to sleep. I laid among them and, gazing sleepily at them, I fell asleep as well. It was wonderful to sleep next to female bodies again, even if just for the warmth and not for the sexual gain, but when I woke up, they were gone.

Months ago, I came back to life somehow. I was flesh and blood and bones again. I lived in the city for few months, scrounging the streets and doing a shitty job. But I couldn't find my purpose anymore. *Why did she leave me? Why did she let me go?*

It has been one year, one day, and exactly one hour

now since I've been living on this goddamn mountain. Since the last time I saw a human being. It could be more. I might be mistaken. Time has a funny way of passing through here.

They say a city is part of the civilized world, but for me that became more and more clear it was bullshit — a big fat lie to get us all to buy into their consumerism, to fill their pockets with money and the planet with toxic shit we don't really need. I saw drug dealers at every corner in my district, arms dealers and rubbish littered the streets; the putrefied smell was suffocating.

So I came to the mountain. I sold most of my stuff — the little I had — and, only with a large backpack in which I saved my essentials, I headed over here to live in a yurt. Two good university friends helped me put it up and there I was: all setup to live like a mountain man.

The first three days were pure bliss. I listened to the stream trickle through the old sharp stones, the wild birds playing in the trees, I even saw a pack of wild pigs one night. They were so loud, at first I though there was an earthquake. The earth was trembling under their heavy bodies. But that didn't scare me. In fact, it filled me with excitement and a sense of adventure. I thought maybe, just maybe, I could actually feel like *living* again.

I was ready and eager to embrace everything. Until the third night, when I heard old men's voices outside my yurt. The nearest neighbor was a monk who lived in a tiny earth house about two kilometers away from my place. I doubted it was him. He was a kind man. I grabbed an old sword I had kept from my father, a gift he had given me before he passed away, and ventured to the door. Holding the sword tightly, I listened.

Sooner or later you will diiiie. Just... hooow....the decision is being voted... riiight now.

My heart jumped in my chest. My breathing accelerated. The trees outside creaked and turned. Branches rustled in the wind.

Die...How...die...how...how would you liiike to diiie? the voices said.

I tensed my fingers round the sword and thought quickly.

Who the fuck wants me dead? And what am I going to do to save myself?

I looked around in my yurt. I had a fire I could use to my defense, but I could lose my home if I were to throw any burning embers and wood at the furious men shouting outside. The yurt could catch fire and I couldn't afford that. Winter was soon coming.

The only weapons I had were a small knife, used for cutting vegetables, and the sword. But I didn't know how to use them well, not for fighting. They had been more for decor than for protection. I cracked the door slowly and looked out, not exactly ready to face a bunch of angry men. When I peaked my head out, I was stunned. Dozens of females, wearing only see-through shawls and nothing else, were sleeping just outside my yurt again, in the circle of stones. Mesmerized, but still staring in all directions, looking for the angry voices, I approached them. A sudden sleep took over me and I fell between two of them.

The next night, I heard the furious voices again. And a shattering, crackling, earth-moving noise. I rushed outside terrified, sword in hand, ready to strike. There was nobody. Only an owl, sitting on a tree branch. He stared at me curiously. I frowned and scanned the area. Nobody in sight. *What the hell is going on? Am I having nightmares? Is there an actual earthquake this time?* I thought in haste and grumbled in frustration. I came to the mountain to find some sort of peace. *This was not it.* I sighed.

I brushed my tired eyes and went back inside. I listened for a little longer to the wild noises outside, but it turned eerily quiet. Even the wind was silent. I got into my sturdy bed, wondering why the hell was I so scared. The city had turned me into a useless man — a joke — unable to take care of myself if necessary. I swore I was going to be a better man and dozed off fifteen minutes later.

I looked for tracks the next day. They were there plenty, all right. Dozens and dozens of tracks going round and round my yurt. I frowned. Someone wanted to scare me, maybe even hurt me, if the voices I heard spoke the truth. And then I blacked out.

I woke up next to a fire. My hands and feet were tied to a wooden cross and dry branches were nested at my feet. Old men were staring at me whispering words in a language I didn't recognize. Words I couldn't make out. I couldn't understand them, but their actions were clear: they were about to burn me alive. I began shouting and struggling against the wooden cross, trying my hardest to escape. It was futile. The rope they tied me with was too thick to break with my own hands. They flicked a match and lit the fire under my feet. I began to scream louder. Then suddenly, from hot, excruciating pain, my body was hit with sharp chunks of ice. You would think I welcomed the cold, and I did, *at first*. But soon, it become obvious things were getting worse. You see, somehow the ice chunks didn't melt when they made contact with my body; in fact, at impact with my chest, they struck excruciating cold, and nestled well inside my body. They stuck out from me, trickles of blood streaming down my chest. I must have looked like a stuffed human puppet to them.

A terrifying thought took over me. *They aren't just trying to kill me, they are torturing me first.*

Through the flames, I saw the smiles plastered on their faces. But they weren't actually smiling — no, they were crying, their cheeks glistening with tears.

Forgive us, the voices whispered at unison. *Please forgive us, son.*

I squirmed in pain.

"Let me go. It's not too late," I yelled. My hair was charred, the soles of my feet covered in burns and blisters. The sharp ice still pushed at my chest. It seemed colder than before.

I'm sorry.

They stuffed my mouth with soil, worms writhing in it, reaching for my tongue, my throat.

"Please," I tried, "please don't do this."

One of the old men pulled out a rat from a sack. Two others forced my mouth open, and the old man held the rat from its tail and dangled it above my mouth, teasing the animal. My eyes bulged, dropping hot tears, but however much I tried, I couldn't shut my mouth. The man dropped the rat into my mouth. He rushed towards my throat, scratching my tongue, running famished and eager towards my insides. I began choking. I peed myself and cried, praying for death to come and get me already.

I woke up in my bed, covered in sweat and piss. My whole body shuddered, still within the grasps of the nightmare, the fear and the horror I had felt so vividly. When I realized I was back in my yurt, unscathed, I laughed loudly and ashamed at myself.

I removed my clothes and started to get rid of the mess I had made. *What the hell is wrong with me?* I mumbled to myself. *Have I picked the wrong wild mushrooms to cook?*

A loud bang hit my door then. I shook with fear. The bed was pissed already. I put one foot on the floor, and then the other. My legs were trembling. I glanced at the wall. The sword was gone. I panicked. I don't know why, but instead of grabbing the small knife I had, I've put my own hand into the fire and grabbed a few burning charcoals. I rushed toward the door, ready to strike and burn whoever was outside. You can easily say that was stupid, I wouldn't disagree. Not that I think a knife would have made a difference in favor of my fate, but still.

Nothing else strange happened for 6 months until then, as I told you already. Those thirteen asleep women appeared again. And then, few nights after their appearance, old men's voices began again outside my door, surrounding my yurt, threatening me. So after that… nightmare, I didn't know what to make of it all. I rushed out scared, furious at my own fear, and determined to have my say to whomever turned out to be outside yelling and threatening me. The forest had become my home, I did not want to be forced out of it. In my mind, I intended to defend myself and stay on my ground. But that turned out to be a poor choice of words inside my head.

With burning embers in my hand, I opened the door.

The eerily soft wind enveloped me, and the same owl from the other night glanced at me again.

You foool...You really think you could face US? Chilling voices shouted at me, the terrifying sounds coming from nowhere and everywhere *at once.*

A peculiar purple light shone on me, illuminating my entire body. It fascinated me. I stood still as a statue. Embers burned my palm. I dropped them to the ground. I forgot about that pain as soon as a dagger was thrust into my chest. At least, that's how it felt like. Instead of a dagger though, an invisible hand — an invisible force, maybe powered by the strange, hypnotic light — ripped my heart out. I was *literally heartless*. The ravaged area of my upper body began to burn. Flames were leaping from the outer edges of my torn skin. I didn't understand how I was still alive. But I felt *everything*. Little black birds came rushing out from where my organ used to be, flapped their wings, and flew joyfully around me and towards the sky. Their wings looked like they were on fire too, but they weren't actually. Orange light shone from *within* them.

There was a strange sensation in my chest — in my entire body. I knew I was dead, and yet, I felt like I wasn't.

I dropped on my knees and fell on the ground covered with a thin layer of decomposed leaves. Thick roots from the trees came at me, pocking and jabbing and pinching at my body, wrapping it like in a cocoon. I could feel myself losing air. Dying, yet living somehow. The roots wrapped me tighter. As my eyes were closing, I could barely make out the outline of the owl. He was going back to sleep.

The trees creaked and swayed with the wind, as if in a grandiose dance, all, together as one.

You fooool... nooow.... and forever... we'll taaake... caaare... of youuuu...

The wind brushed through the trees, whistled, and carried the whispers away.

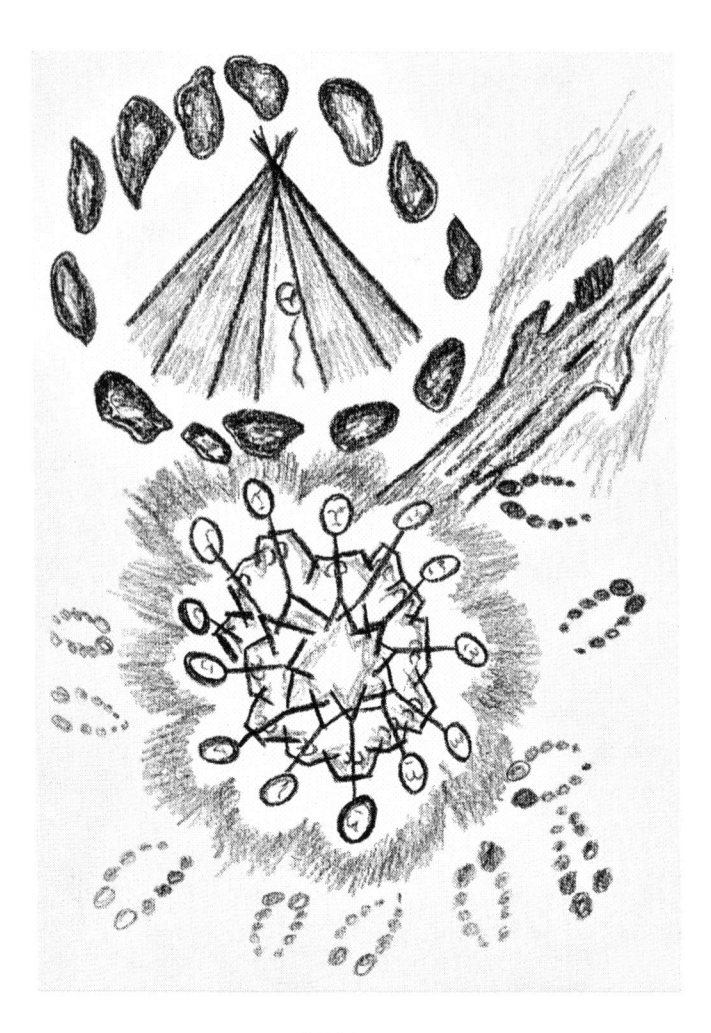

Whispers

Pricolici

I had been walking on my own for three days when I saw it. The creature stood perched on the cliff, stared at the moon and then started howling. From that distance, I could only see its silhouette, but it was large enough to make me fear it. I checked to see if my knife was still in its place and checked my surroundings. I had to find a place to hide. But where? It was almost dusk and I could tell the forest was getting thicker the more I advanced. I decided to set my tent at the base of few large beech trees. I pondered whether to light a fire or not. I was afraid the animal was going to be attracted by it and come in my direction.

I decided against it.

I thought about what I saw earlier. I was aware that a large population of wolves still lived in this country so I had expected to see one in one of these hikings. To be honest with you, I actually wanted to see one close. It was exhilarating to see an animal like this in the wild. But I had not expected it to be this large. I was slightly worried but happy I had some weapons to protect myself with. I presumed I should be fine in my tent and fell asleep.

I woke up early in the morning. The grass was covered with a thick dew and the earth smelled fresh, alive. I stretched, made myself some simple food — couscous with dried vegetables and chillies — to keep me going. I cleaned after myself and gathered my tent. I carried on walking. I had to find her. I expected to be near the property by now. For all I knew, I might have actually been inside it by then. I hadn't seen a sign or whatever, but I knew the forest was part of the land she owned. It was a massive property, several hectares of wild landscape surrounded me. I saw several squirrels and rabbits on my way here but now I was deeper into the forest. I expected to see deers soon. Just as I thought about the wonderful form of these animals, the smell of fresh blood hit my nostrils and there, few meters ahead of me, laying on the forest ground, was a large stag, or at least what was left of it. I looked around me but there was no sign of the killer. It was probably gone by now. The poor animal had been mostly ripped apart, viciously consumed. There was blood splattered on a few stinging nettles and other wild plants around it where it had found its ending. I said a silent prayer and continued my walk, more aware of my surroundings and quite shaken by the bloody sight. I had seen dead animals before, but this was something else. I could barely shake the remains of the stag from my mind when I stumbled upon an even more horrifying sight. The head of a wolf, torn from its body, was just at my feet, hidden by wild plants. I almost stepped on it. I shrieked in revulsion when I saw the bloodied fangs, but breathed in relief when I realized the animal was dead and couldn't harm me. But then the sudden realization hit me: who had killed the wolf? What other creatures lurked in this forest? Was I in danger, more danger than I had anticipated? Well, that was still to be decided, but I was obviously in a little bit over my head by now. I started to regret the decision to come over here to this foreign place to do my research. The lady's offer to host me, to give me a place to stay while I looked for the flower — for answers — had been kind though and I couldn't refuse it. I was also intrigued by it, I have to admit. *Why the letter? Why me?*

I practiced my breathing, trying to calm down my beating heart, saying to myself that I was only overreacting. I was in a foreign land. I just had to get accustomed with the place. Surely finding dead animals here and there was just the natural order around here. I was in the wilderness, after all. I just had to find her home and convince her to be my guide in these parts. *Everything will fall into place then.* Sure enough as I thought about those things, a massive castle came into view and I was more than happy when I reached the long bridge and walked across it, arriving at the main gate. I had arrived at my destination. I knocked three times as advised in my letter and waited. The head of a large wolf was carved in dark stone and adorned the main entrance. It looked intimidating, but nonetheless, the artwork was as impressive as it was frightening. I marveled at it and took a photograph. After several minutes of waiting, a young man opened the gate and after inspecting me briefly, he allowed me inside.

We had a nice dinner, me and the lady of the castle.
After I finished eating, I started making conversation. The truth is, I really wanted to spend the night with her, make her mine, you know. She gave me the impression that she could be a delicious lover. And she seemed into me as well. Who doesn't like that, eh?
"You should come visit me sometimes," I said.
"I have everything I need here."
"Yeah, but don't you want to see the world from time to time?"
"I cannot leave this place," she said, annoyed.

"Look, the truth is, it would be nice to come visit you and all that, see your part of the world, but I can't. I am bound to this castle by a curse," she said bluntly.

"What do you mean? What curse?"

"On every week with a full moon, on every night of that week when the moon is completely filled with light, my body turns into a beast. *I* turn into a beast. For four nights, I run these forests and look for prey. I do not sleep, I do not rest. I run wild. I am a savage creature, unable to control myself.

"If I were to leave this place," she continued, "on the next full moon I would turn again into the creature, but from then onward, I would remain as the creature forever. So you see, I cannot leave. I cannot take that chance. Not unless I want to stay a beast forever. And I don't."

I frowned and was left speechless at this shared secret. I didn't know what to do or say.

"I inherited the castle from my grandfather. I grew up here and he took care of me when I was little. He knew what was waiting for me. It was the least he could do, he said, building this castle for me, to keep *me* protected. He still runs these forests at night. *Every night*. All he did was protect me from what happened to him."

"What happened to him?"

Just as she was about to answer me, a ferocious howl erupted from the forest.

"I have to go," she said.

"But..."

"I'll see you later. I'll come to you."

"As a beast or as a —"

"Just be patient," she snapped. She then smiled and walked away.

I made fun of the situation because I wasn't sure if she was serious. Maybe it was the Romanian sarcasm. Maybe she just wanted to make fun of me. Scare me that I could be eaten by a beast in her forest. See what I would do, if I was game or not for a little bit of fun. Or maybe it was her way of telling me to *fuck off, I don't want to sleep with you.* Somehow though, I didn't feel like she was joking. She was serious. But how could that be?

Yeah, *sure*, Dracula, werewolves, vampires, spirits, ghouls — all these sort of creatures are entertaining, but they aren't actually real. I don't believe they are.

I even heard about a creature larger than a regular wolf — *a Pricolici*. Similar to a werewolf, but different. Apparently, a Pricolici — name used both for singular and plural — was once a bad man who died and came back again from his grave as a beast, to continue to cause havoc and to harm humans.

Anyway, all these make for a fun read and great dinner conversations, but really. *Come on.* Things like these don't exist. They're just inventions of various writers who want to turn folklore stories into a buck. Or at best, they're stories used to raise the tourism in someone's country. *That's all.* Scientists haven't found actual proof of anything like this, which proves my point again.

But what if there was something to all of this? What if she was — *she is* — a beast? I scrubbed the thought away as I was walking up the stone stairs to the room I was given. I undressed and took a shower. I dried myself with a towel and walked back into the room. I was still drying my hair when I saw her. There she was, laying on my bed — *her bed technically.*

I gazed at her and smirked. I should have been embarrassed maybe, I was completely naked after all. But so was she. I considered it equal ground, even if this was her castle.

"Aren't you worried you're going to devour me?"

"Aren't *you*?"

"Well, the way you look right now, you can do all the devouring you want. I'll take my chances. Besides, it's not a full moon yet," I said, teasing.

She smiled wickedly.

We made love. When I woke up the next morning, she was already gone.

I had hoped she would be my guide, but instead she disappeared for days. She left word to be given everything I need and to be fed properly. She provided me with a strong horse as well, and a young man accompanied me while I was doing my research in the forest, looking for the flower. But I wanted her company. After that night, I couldn't think much of my research, I couldn't think much of anything else but her. Her body on mine, pressing into me, raising me over and over… Heh, to think of what she joked about, being a beast and all, made me smile mischievously. I could see what she meant by that. She exhausted me. But it was such sweet surrender.

Still, her absence pained my heart and I waited for her to join me for dinner every evening. On a fourth evening, she finally showed her face.

"Where have you been? I've missed you. You've been gone for ages."

"Don't be silly," she said coldly. "I was only gone a little while. I had things to do. You're not the only person I have to take care of, you know."

Her eyes looked gaunt, her lips bruised. *Tense.*

We ate in silence. I refused to have my plate cleaned when I finished and I offered to do it myself instead.

"The least I can do," I said, proud and frustrated.

"Suit yourself," she said. "I'm going to sleep."

"You do that. It looks like you need it," I replied, bitter.

She frowned at me, then smiled a little. She was gone quickly and I was left cleaning. Her staff offered to do the job for me, but I refused. After I finished, I went to sleep.

She woke me up at 2 in the morning. She snuggled next to me in bed. I wanted to turn and face her, tell her to get the hell out of my bed. *Her bed.* Instead, I felt the warmth of her naked body and I surrendered to the pleasure. I knew what she was about to do and my whole body waited in anticipation for her moves.

I woke up alone again. This kept happening for a few more nights, until I decided I was going to follow her and find out where she was disappearing to. I shouldn't have done that. I should have done my research and left, went back to where I was coming from. But I didn't.

I followed her through the forest until she went into a cave. I followed her inside as well, but stopped and hid behind a massive rock wall when I saw the beast. It was much larger than a wolf. I would like to say that I was brave and didn't scare easily, but that was hardly the case. I realized I didn't know anyone in these parts, but her and her people, and if I were to get lost or disappear, nobody would know, nobody would find me because nobody knew where to look.

She and the beast were feasting on a deer. Blood

dripped from their fangs and they slashed the poor animal to pieces, with an insatiable desire to consume it fully.

I felt sick to my stomach, but tried to hold it together. I waited. After they ate the animal, they both laid by the fire and fell asleep.

I made my escape then. I ran as fast as I could. As I was running, I realized the moon was high on the sky and it was full. It lit my path well, but it also reminded me of what she had said to me the first evening we had dined together. On every night with a full moon…

I run these forests and look for prey. I do not sleep, I do not rest. I run wild. I am a savage creature, unable to control myself.

The words sent shivers through my body. In my desperation, I stepped on a rock I didn't see and fell to the ground. I had twisted my ankle. I crawled and rested my back on a tree trunk. It looked old enough to have been there since the beginning of time. Or maybe it was just my imagination, running crazy and exaggerating everything that came in my way since I saw them in the cave. I thought I could see a man's face drawn on the tree. It looked twisted, as if in pain. Nettles stung at my feet and animal sounds came rushing. I feared my life was about to end. I caught glimpse of a flower. It grew bigger, right under my eyes. The shape of its petals resembled the claw of a wolf or some sort of carnivorous animal. They were sharp, long, and pointy. There were eyes in the middle of two petals. They stared right at me and sparkled. I shook my head and rubbed my eyes. *It's just the moonshine, you fool... it can't be...* The flower grew a little bit more and a mouth emerged within its structure. Absentmindedly, I sniffed some of the black and red powder held within the mouth-looking-petals. When I realized what happened — what I did — it was too late. It had already bit me. I stumbled like I was drunk and fell.

A soft voice whispered prayers. I opened my eyes. She sat by my bedside, holding my hand in hers, kissing it. I pulled it away.

"You're awake. How are you feeling? Don't make any abrupt moves. You've had an allergic reaction to a plant and most of your body is covered in bites and bruises."

"What? What do you mean...?" I began to say, but then the pain hit, just as I tried to move my feet.

"What plant? I've never been allergic. Never. To anything."

"There's always a first time, darling. And this is a rare plant, so it's unlikely you've ever encountered it before," she said, softly.

"But I saw..."

"What did you see? Tell me."

"Ahhh...nothing. I must have been hallucinating. What I saw... it couldn't be... hm...that's impossible."

"This plant you've found does give bad dreams, on top of the physical pain. But whatever you saw, rest assured, you're safe. It never happened. Just a construct of your imagination."

"I must have a terrible imagination," I mumbled. "So... where's this flower? I want to—"

"I've destroyed it, of course. It almost killed you," she said. "Do you have a death wish or something?"

"No, of course not, but it was my life's work, that's why I came here, to—"

"Here, have some tea then. It will make you feel better. It always works. Takes the pain away instantly. Like it was never there in the first place. And forget about the flower, it can't hurt you anymore. *No more nightmares*."

I smiled, bitterly, drank the tea and hoped for the best. All I wanted was the pain to be gone. To be my old self again. She held my hand and I fell asleep again.

When I woke up again, she was standing by the window. Morning light painted her face clear and fresh. But then I noticed something that wasn't there before. Her belly was swollen.

"What happened?"

She turned and smiled.

"What was bound to happen. If you make love to me so often," she said bluntly, teasing me.

I frowned. "But the last time I saw you, that... wasn't there. And now it's...there."

"The last time you saw me?"

"Just yesterday, when I woke up from the allergic reaction..."

"Oh, not this again. Darling, come on. We've been through this before. Your allergic reaction, that happened a long time ago."

Shocked, I stared at her. "How long ago?"

"A few years back. Now and then, you still get this thing, when you think you've just woken up from a terrible nightmare caused by the plant, the flower you were looking for. Your life's research. And I have to bring you back to reality. But I don't mind. You're a great lover, if you know what I mean," she said, winking at me, "so if that's the price I have to pay, I'll pay it dearly. Over and over again. You gave me this," she said, rubbing her belly and smiling at me with tears in her eyes. "I can't be grateful to you enough."

Sure enough, I looked under the covers and saw my body fitter than ever, stronger than ever. I brushed away the dark thoughts haunting my mind, the beasts I thought I saw, and took her hand in mine. I kissed it.

"You're right. I remember now," I said. *At least, I think I do. I do, yes. I've always wanted her, since the first moment I saw her in the castle. How strange, I was never so sure about anything in my entire life. I loved her then, and I do now. I always will. Somehow, I know this for sure, with certitude.*

"Come here," I said, and kissed her hands. Thanks for keeping me safe."

She smiled and gently caressed her belly.

The child was born few days later. I was asked to wait outside the entire time, and I didn't mind. I could hear her cries and struggle. She was in a lot of pain. I worried she might not make it and all sorts of horrible thoughts came through my mind. *How am I going to raise a baby on my own, if something happens to her? I know nothing about kids. I am an only child.*

A small howl came from the room she was giving birth in. I tensed and knocked on the door.

"Everything ok?"

"Everything is just perfect. We have made a son."

I laughed, relieved and happy that everything was over with. She was safe.

"Isn't he all you ever wished for?" she said.

I gazed into the eyes of the newborn boy. He gazed back. I felt a pain in my left side and frowned.

"You ok?" she said, looking at me, worried.

"I guess I'm a bit under the weather, or just getting old. Who knows. Time comes to us all to take its share," I said, serious.

"But I'm a father now," I said, gleefully. "And to think I was told I could never have kids. This is a miracle."

I kissed the baby's forehead and his eyes sparkled.

Pricolici

In the Dream

He slept again on the wrong side of his body. We had been sleeping together for about ten years and during this entire period, he always slept on his right side. Until three nights ago when suddenly, he shifted his weight from right to left. I looked at him in the dark and wondered. *Listened.* I found it strange, but I just told myself I was being ridiculous, imagining things that weren't there. Reading and writing no sleep stories made me question every shadow, every mumble. I made something strange appear from everywhere and nowhere, just to make a scary story. So I ignored the weird feeling and dozed off.

The next night he did the same. I listened again, unable to contain myself. His breath was warm. He mumbled and shook in his sleep. But he often shook when he slept. I learned to deal with that along the years. I thought maybe he was having another one of his out of body experiences. So I gently massaged his back and he quickly settled into peaceful sleep again. The fact he slept on his left, facing me, was still strange to me. But it was 4:39 in the morning and I hadn't slept since 9 the previous morning. I slumped my head onto my pillow and attempted to sleep.

Then, the mumbling started again. I could only make out a few words, but hearing them uttered from his mouth scared the crap out of me. I couldn't shut one eye for the rest of the morning. I waited for him to wake up and go to work.

What was going on? Why was he whispering those words? I memorized them and looked up for translation online.

From what I could find out — which wasn't much — he was talking with someone. *He was having a conversation.*

I will help you, he whisper-mumbled in his sleep.

I will help you get her. He laughed out-loud then, which in the silence of the night made it all more strange and frightening, but he still didn't wake up. The hairs stood up on my arms, on guard.

I asked him about the dream later that evening when he come back from work, but he said he didn't remember a thing. He usually was great at remembering his dreams. One more red flag. I refused to sleep with him. I was too freaked out. I went to sleep on the small couch in the living room instead. He came to me in the middle of the night, feeling sorry for keeping me awake the previous night, and begged me to go to sleep with him. He teased me with caresses and kisses. I should have known better, but I took the wrong decision. I went with him.

After we made love, we went back to rest. He fell asleep immediately. Our love making was efficient. We had used up our energy. Our strength was in little portions now.

After 20 minutes, he started moving slightly, and he mumbled something. I couldn't quite get it at first, the words were twisted, as if the letters were inversed. I couldn't understand him. But they became clear soon after.

The man in the dream... He's trying to... stab me. He wants my heart, he mumbled. *But I won't give it to him,* he said again. I froze and failed to go back to sleep. I watched over him the rest of the morning. For a brief moment that night, he flexed his fingers and grabbed my arm tightly. I struggled a bit under his strong fingers, and my arm hurt where he grabbed me, but it was nothing bad I couldn't get over, nothing I couldn't handle. I rubbed the area and the pain was soon gone. I thought back to a film I once helped on when I was at university. It was about a man who was violent with his girlfriend while he slept. I frowned and shivered. But then I calmed down. That was *just* a film. He would never hurt me. *He's a kind man. He's the best thing that happened to me.* But I did fear those nightmares he had, or whatever they were. I worried.

I smiled and gently rubbed his arms. I kissed his warm skin and leaned my head on his chest. I watched over him as he slept. He usually snored, which made it harder for me to fall asleep, but that night he didn't. He slept peacefully.

I must've dozed off for a few seconds. When I woke up, my hair and my hand were smudged with something wet. It smelled funny, *strange*. I didn't recognize it at first. I've never seen that much of it in one place, let alone having actual physical contact with it. But then I turned on the lamp and I saw it better.

Once, when I was seven or eight years old and prepping food for the ducks in my yard, I almost chopped off my left index finger. I still have the scar to this day. I'll take it to the ground with me, it's never gonna go away. I bled a lot that day, so much that a pool of blood gathered in a white-brownish bowl beside me which was meant for the little ducks' food. It was my first ever encounter with the alive red liquid. But I've never seen that much of it like on his chest that night. It was running in rivulets. His black hair was glistening with sweat. His thick eyebrows were twitching. His eyes were closed. And then he settled. He stopped moving.

His T-shirt and the top of his chest were completely soaked and stained with blood. When they moved him, the white bed sheet that was on the bed that night got smudged even more. The mattress too. It looked like someone stabbed him with something, but there was no weapon anywhere to be found. They claim I hid it and then got rid of it somehow, but that's not true. He just went to sleep, and someone — *something* — did that to him. He never woke up again since then. He just lies there, on that bed, not dead, but not alive either.

Although they can't prove it, they still tarnish my name on social channels and say that most likely I did it — that perhaps I tried to kill him in a fit of jealousy and somehow I managed to do that without leaving a weapon behind, but that's a mistake — a misunderstanding. I would never hurt him. Why would I do that to the one I love? I wouldn't. It makes no sense whatsoever.

And he, too, lies there, comfortably, and there's a smile on his face. It makes me smile as well.

In the Dream

The Staircase

I was standing in the middle of a staircase. My knees were weak. I steadied myself by taking hold of the polished balustrade. To my right and to my left and all around me there were steps leading to different paths on the staircase. I was to discover they were all leading to the same place. But I didn't know then. I only had my suspicions, my suppositions. What was to happen if I took the wrong turn? Was I going to fall into oblivion, disappear into the darkness, never to be seen, never found? I stepped carefully and scanned the area. But it was dark around me, I couldn't see far. The Staircase was the only way. The more I walked, the more I saw. It was deeply quiet. I could hear the echo of silence. There was nobody around I could ask for directions.

I ascended and descended. The steps creaked under my bare feet. There were dozens of broken mirrors on the walls. In one of them, there was blood dripping from my arms, but I looked at myself — checked my body — and there was nothing of the sort. My skin was fine. I frowned, disturbed by that sight, but kept on going.

Every now and then, I reached a door. The first one I opened, tired of all the walking up and down, revealed a most painful sight: a woman was kneeling on the floor. Dark hair was cascading on her shoulders. She was screaming, arguing, shouting vile words, her mouth twisting, contorting, unstopping. A man was on top of her. His hands wrapped around her neck and squeezed. Suddenly, he glanced at the opened door and saw me.

He stopped instantly. He let her go just as I had slammed the door shut.

I started trembling. My hands and feet shook uncontrollably.

I crawled into a ball by the dingy mirror wall, as if I was six years old again, and sobbed for a while. I picked myself up and tried the door again. It seemed to be locked from the outside. But there was no key laying around to open it. I looked under the rugged carpet — nothing. I listened carefully, heart pounding in my chest, but I couldn't hear another noise coming from the inside of that room.

A few moments later, I steadied my feet and started walking again. There was another door about ten feet in front of me. I disregarded it but the same door appeared again. I ignored it again and again it appeared. I opened it slowly. A slim, old man was laying on a bed, touching himself. The sheets were yellow and the room smelled of old dirty clothes and horse manure. There was this skinny legged girl, eleven or twelve years of age, propped uncomfortably with her head on a pillow, next to him. She sat still, unaware of what was about to happen. He took her hand and moved it down. She stood frozen, like a conscious being stuck in a puppet's body. She saw a younger girl peeking through a window, wanting to go in; she rushed to close the curtain as if to say, 'Don't look, don't come inside. Stay *away* from him!'. The man glanced menacing at the door, but I shut it before he had a chance to catch a look at my face.

By now, my forehead was covered in beads of sweat and my palms were clammy, my knuckles white.

Another door appeared. I wanted to ignore it, but I already knew what would happen if I did that, so I went and pushed the handle. A young man stood by a fireplace. Charcoals were burning brightly. His face was warm, his dark eyes sparkled in the firelight, and he had a kind smile as he stared at the flames. There was the shape of a teenage girl standing on a bed nearby, almost shielded by darkness. He looked up and smiled at her. She smiled back. He went and caressed her face with his soft hands, gazing closely into her eyes. As he took her hand in his, a single, curved red line started to show on his arm and he began to bleed profusely from his right wrist. Startled, I backed down and, in my haste, I knocked over a bowl full with red apples that was on a small table, also in the dark. The apples fell to the wooden floor, spreading everywhere. Some of them were rotten. Broken pieces and their sticky juice smeared the floor. Tears started to fall down my face and kept on falling. I shut the door quietly, yet I could still hear its echo.

I ran on the old staircase, up and down, up and down for what felt like hours, trying to find an exit, a window towards the light. I refused to open another door. But then I grew tired. Another door appeared. I gave in and opened it. Willow tree branches of a vivid yellow-green brightened and brushed my face gently. A middle-aged woman was hastily running towards some plum trees at the back of a house. She had a rope in her hand. She was crying. She seemed drained and determined to leave, to—

A man pulled her close. He grabbed her arm and threw away the rope. She sobbed at his chest. I shuddered and closed the door. Tears were streaming down my cheeks, unstoppable. A pain in my temples and forehead was killing me.

I understood then, finally. This staircase was my hell. I was reliving my worst memories, over and over again. What could have been, what should have been. What happened and what didn't. What still could. Possibilities. Life. Death. Memories. *Choices.*

I wanted it to end. Was this how it was going to be all the time? I wished I had a button to turn everything off.

I pounded on the doors. One by one, they flew open. The rooms were all empty now, covered in thick dust. Spiders crawled around. There was nothing I could do. I was all alone. Just me and the dust. And the fucking headache.

I ran to one of the mirror walls and slammed my head into it. The mirror broke into pieces. They fell loudly to the floor. Most of the glass pieces broke further, but one was large enough. I picked it up. I began to cut. My wrist started to bleed. The blood started to cover the floor in small drops. I continued to cut, horizontally and vertically — a twisted T, starting from my left wrist, continuing higher up, towards my elbow. I began to bleed out quickly, streaks of blood running down my hands. I could hear the echo of the drops falling on the dim lit staircase. Like drops of water, falling into a bucket, only thicker.

I descended in complete darkness, all the way to the bottom of the staircase. I didn't know how I got there, but I had a pretty clear idea. It started all over again. I ascended and descended the stairs. The same doors appeared. Over and over again. I stood at the top, pondering what to do. Sharp pain ticked in my head like a time bomb ready to blow up. My heart was pounding.

I stepped slowly towards the edge and threw myself at the darkness — embraced it. The spiral staircase twisted, and twisted, and twisted. I briefly saw an open chest filled with books, a few scattered on the floor, some still falling, suspended in the air, surrounded by darkness. A single light shone on them. There was a petite woman, with snow-white hair, wrinkled skin and a kind smile, gazing at me. My heart slowed down a bit, but then the staircase continued to twist and twirl, dizzying me. I fell.

I landed with a thud — abrupt and silent. I woke up on a bed. There were some thick trees outside my window. The sheets on my bed were pure white, almost hurting my eyes with their brightness. I grabbed my head in my palms and started swaying. I twirled some of my black long hair around my finger and ripped a few strands. I continued swaying. I kept pulling and ripping my hair as if I was analyzing and dissecting each strand to its molecular formation, aware of the damage I was causing, but unable to stop.

I had a fuzzy yet somehow clear thought that I had killed myself, or tried to. I never wanted to go this way. I wanted to live. I wanted to know how the story was going to end. I had things to finish. I didn't want to give up. I didn't even want to say it out loud, what I felt when I thought about that staircase, what I saw, how I finished. I didn't say it out loud. I didn't want to admit it, but it felt... real. It had... happened. Or maybe it didn't. *No*, surely I didn't go through with it. Maybe I thought about it but—

There was a young child somewhere near, I had the faintest idea — the vision — that there was a young daughter present in my life, or was going to be. I didn't know where to find the baby though. And there was a man too, I was certain. I had no idea where he was, but I wasn't that worried about him. I knew he was going to be fine somehow, even if he might have already been dead by then. But I didn't think he was. *He lived on.*

Rays of morning sun hit the Victorian windows — or at least what looked Victorian to me — through the pine trees. The sleeping white gown I had on felt clean and soft. I stopped pulling and ripping my hair. I stood up, went to the window and gazed closer at the pine trees swaying in the wind. The sun shone through the sharp pointy needles. The strong branches swayed and swayed and swayed, as in a simple, magical and wonderful dance. I smiled weakly and opened the window. The wind blew gently and caressed my face. The pain was gone — *for now*. The deep dark green of the trees filled my eyes. This was *just another day.*

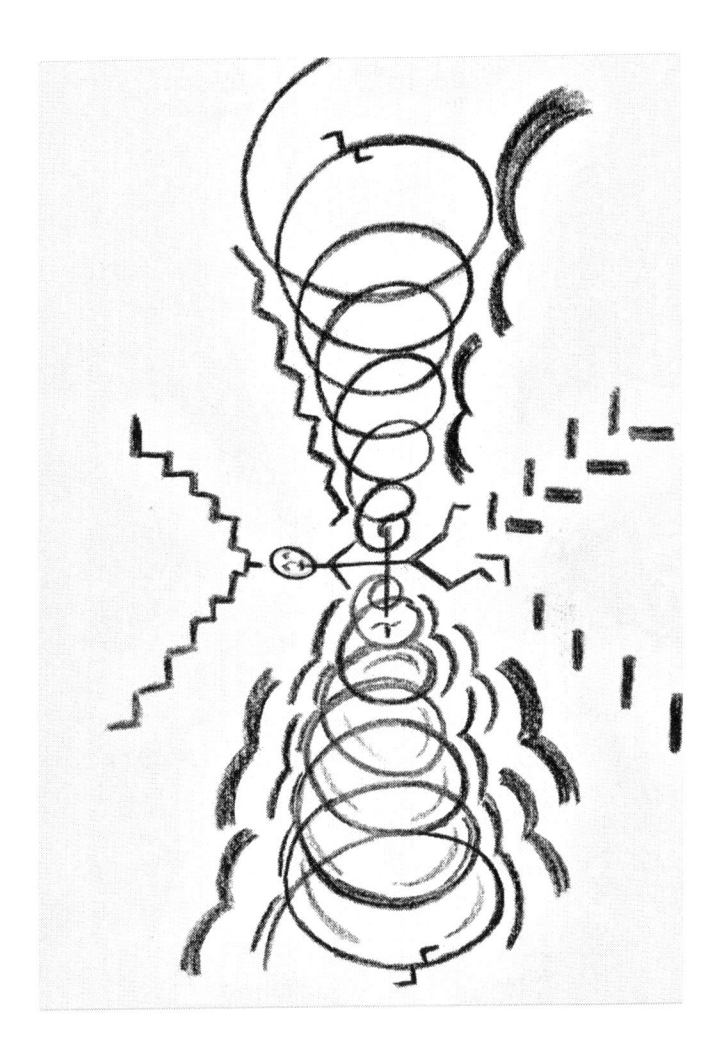

The Staircase

The Man in the Snow

I woke up in the early hours of the morning. The streets were covered in white. The snow fell quietly upon them, upon the skyscrapers. There was a man standing just outside my building, leaning on the light pole, near the old tunnel sprayed in graffiti underneath the railway. He stood still and was staring directly at my window. At first, I thought I was imagining him, seeing a face where it was just a weird pattern on the metal pole. After all, I lived on the 6th floor and there was some distance to the ground, to the street. But the more I looked, the more I saw, his eyes and mouth twisted in anger, his fists clutched tight. It was then when I noticed he held something — a shiny object. I couldn't quite tell what it was from that distance. It looked like a stick or a wand, but I couldn't be sure. I held some comfort that he couldn't possibly see me in the dark, with the lights all shut in my apartment. He was probably just looking at the building, not particularly at me. And yet, I wondered... *What did he see? What was he staring at so intently? Why was he angry? And why was he outside on this weather in the first place?*

The snow fell swiftly and steady. It was coming down nicely. It hadn't snowed in ages, it was a pretty sight. I looked back at the metal pole, but the man was gone. Maybe I had imagined him. All these late nights, early mornings, playing with my own sanity, my own health, can't possibly be good for my eyes either. I went back to bed.

I woke up late in the afternoon. The streets were all white. I expected the snow to be melted by now, knowing the typical weather in this country. But the snow was still here, gracing me with its pretty sight. It snowed like in a fairy tale. I made a cup of peppermint tea, gazed through the window for a couple of minutes, and then I went to my computer. I had to finish the project soon. It was due in a few days. I wrote for several hours and by the time I stood up, it was dark outside. But the snow was still falling, heavily and quietly. I was glad I worked from home and didn't have to embrace the cold to get to an office. It was one thing to look at the snow from inside, and another to walk through it every day.

I took a piss, washed my hands, and made another cup of tea. I returned to my computer. I started writing again. By the time I stood up again, my stomach was growling. I realized I hadn't eaten that day. I frowned and went to make myself a toastie sandwich. As I walked towards the kitchen, I took another peek at the snow. And then I saw him — the same man from before. He was standing outside my building again. This time, he looked happier. But he still held something in his hands and there was something about his face... something wrong, but I couldn't figure out what. My stomach growled again demanding some food, anything. As I picked various ingredients to cook from the fridge, a strange thought occurred to me: *were there any footprints in the snow?* I couldn't remember seeing any, and certainly, there should be some. Sure enough, as I looked through the window, I saw the man again, still standing in the same place. But no footprints. Maybe the snow had covered them by now. *Maybe.* I thought maybe I should call the police, maybe he was a drug addict, or a homeless person who needed help. He must have been really cold standing there like this, with the snow falling on him nonstop. I wondered why he didn't look for shelter under the old tunnel. I had seen people gathering there for a smoke before. He could have slept in there for the night. Even if the floor was littered with infected needles, empty beer cans, broken cardboard and discolored magazine pages, and even if from certain areas in the ceiling there were weeds hanging over, it was a better, safer place than under the free falling snowstorm which was descending slowly, but surely.

And then he vanished — right under my eyes, in a blink. It was like his body disappeared under the snow. I couldn't see him anymore. It was like he had never been there in the first place. I stared at the metal pole covered in snow and wondered for minutes.

Man, I really need to take better care of myself, otherwise, I might start seeing an army of strangers — of zombies — outside my building. I laughed at myself, ironic as always, but frowned and considered some options.

As soon as I get done with the project, I'll start with a better, healthier routine. This couldn't go on forever. Writing until 5 am, waking up late, not eating properly, not taking my pills, not even drinking much water. A cup or two of tea a day was hardly proper and sustainable. I promised to be more careful and went back to writing.

When I finally finished, I looked through the window again. The snow had stopped. I looked back at the metal pole. It was just a metal pole, no strange faces on it, just a shiny metal covered partly in white. I turned to go to sleep, but with the corner of my eye, I noticed something in the communal garden downstairs. It was a shape — a man. He looked up and suddenly started to crawl towards my window. My blood froze and my heart stopped momentarily.

What the fuck? What is that? What's he doing? How is he doing it?

Nonetheless, he kept crawling up, as if he had supernatural powers. The snow started again, more powerful than before. But the man kept going. I started dialing the police, but then I thought what they will say about a man crawling up a building in the middle of a snowstorm. They probably would think it's a bad prank, or that I'm crazy. I couldn't have that again. *No more doctors*. I checked for the window to see if it was locked properly, which it was, and then looked for something to defend myself with in case the man — *the creature* — managed to get inside. Just as I grabbed a large knife from the chopping board, I heard a knock on my window. I turned and saw him staring at me through the clear glass, hit by snow. He looked happy, but his eyes were cold and they weren't like that because of the weather. There was an iciness to them I had never seen in anyone else. He knocked again, *gently*, mocking me. I grabbed the knife tighter in my hand. My heart was beating like crazy, leaping from my chest. He knocked once more. The glass started to crack. Then, I heard a shriek and everything went black.

It is snowing. The flakes are falling quietly and softly on my dark hair, my full lips, my eyes. There is blood too, warm and sticky in the corners of my mouth, but there is more snow. Someone is looking at me from high above. Dawn is soon approaching, I can see the light.

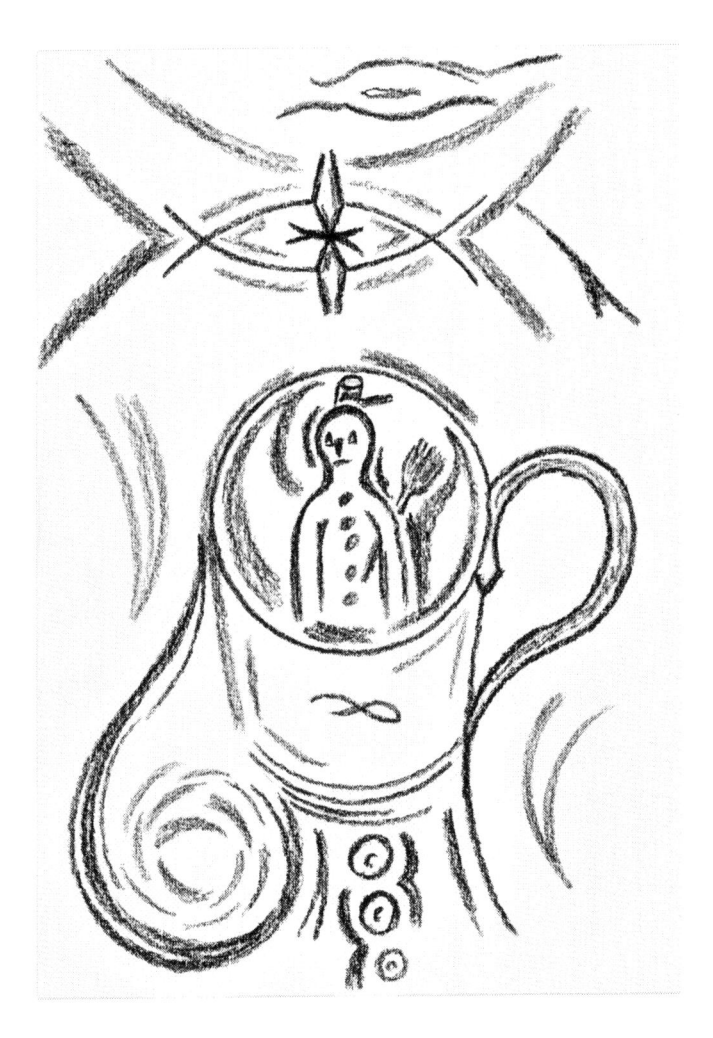

The Man in the Snow

Acknowledgments

Felix Blackwell, for encouraging me to experiment and post my writing on Reddit. This collection of stories wouldn't even exist now if it weren't for your strong advice and captivating stories. *Thank you.*

Florin Vîlsan, for challenging me and for being patient — *thank you*. Here's to our forest.

Vanessa Tavares (aka Psyca), for the wonderful painting. *Obrigada.*

Florin Cristea —dad— for coming up with the inside artwork which you 'just see it, as it should be'. *Mulțumesc.*

Tijs Groen, for the lovely, uplifting music. *Dank je.*

Crystal, Luke, Stacie, Danae, for beta-reading the stories and giving me feedback. *Thank you.*

Alex, for spotting the annoying typos. *Mulțumesc.*

Sufjan Stevens, for the magical music. *Thank you.*

And to **my readers**, old and new, *thank you* for staying with me on this strange ride.

About the Author

Photographs: Florin Vîlsan

Crina-Ludmila Cristea is an independent author. She writes and publishes adult fiction, non-fiction, and kids books.

She is a promoter of a lifestyle as close to nature as possible and plans on having her own food forest — a creative retreat. She occasionally interviews artists and shares their work with the world using her YouTube and other social media channels.

In 2012 she graduated from Canterbury Christ Church University with a degree in Film, Radio, and Television.

In 2016 she published her first non-fiction book about the woodcarving work of her father, and in 2017 she released her first novel (which was banned in Germany, Austria, and Australia for a while). The book was translated into French in 2018.

She is now working on *Midnight Tears* (the sequel to her debut novel), *Tender is the Rain* (a standalone psychological thriller), and other short stories.

Currently, she lives in Manchester, the United Kingdom. She is originally from Vrancea, Romania.

About the Debut Novel

Things, events, and people are not always what they seem to be.

Luke Evans is tirelessly working to make the world a safer place, but when tragedy strikes his family, he is left living a life he's unwilling to embrace.

With his dog as the only companion now, Luke spends his time trying to bury his pain in alcohol and old music, abandoning his goals of making the world a better place. But when a complete stranger knocks on his door, carrying a young baby, Luke unknowingly takes the path to another kind of life.

Peculiar people and events continue to disturb Luke's remote life, changing and peeling it bit by bit. Caught in a reckless existence, with events spiraling out of his control, Luke will find out a terrifying, yet hopeful truth which will give him a renewed purpose.

—

A story of love and loss, with a massive dose of darkness, mystery, and eroticism, *Velvet Touch* will leave a mark bound to last. For adults only.

—

This novel is currently being adapted into a screenplay. The aim with it is to rewrite the story in a less explicit way, one more pleasant for a wider audience, and of course, ultimately, to make it to the big screen.

Film rights have not yet been sold for this book, or for any of the stories in this collection (although offers have been made for an earlier version of what is now *In The Forest of Bluebells*). If you wish to acquire rights to make any of these into a film, please contact the author directly by email.

A Final Note

If you have read this book, please take a few moments to review it.

I'm an independent author which means I write, design, publish, and promote my books (both physical and digital editions). It's tough to make a living doing this, but I've been in love with stories ever since I can remember and I want to share this love with you.

I'm always excited to find out what readers think of my stories. I read and appreciate every single review I get — yes, even the low star ones (they all help me write more and better), so whichever medium you choose to express thoughts and feelings about my stories (Amazon, Instagram, YouTube, *handwritten letters* perhaps), I want you to know your words count and that I thank you for sharing them. It means a lot.

Until next time, stay safe and keep on reading.

Sincerely,

Crina.

23,300 words
Manchester, UK
March, 2019

If you'd like to receive news from me,
GET ON THE LIST|NEVER MISS A BOOK.

https://lilybloomwriter.wixsite.com/officialwebsite

Email: crinalcristea@gmail.com
Instagram: lilybloomwriter
Twitter: lilybloomwriter / CrinaCristea1
stage32.com/profile/676064

40906536R00068

Printed in Poland
by Amazon Fulfillment
Poland Sp. z o.o., Wrocław